Vanished

Six Days in Seven Ways

Kaylynn Hunt

E. Raye Turonek

Toni Larue'

Keira N. James

Tanisha Stewart

Kenya Moss-Dyme

Copyright © 2025

Published by Skylar Publications

ISBN: 979-8-9904480-2-5

Cover Design by Kaylynn Hunt
Edited by T. Denise Black

Printed in the United States of America
First Edition: 2025

Table of Contents

Forward

Everyone who knows me knows I'm always whining about wanting books with alternate endings. I mean, seriously… Why should we only get one version of how things play out when life itself is full of twists, turns, and what-ifs?

Well, one day this idea hit me like a brick to the face. A story so vivid, so wild, so unlike anything I'd personally ever read… And I had to see it come to life. It nagged me for days. So much so that I did what any book nerd with amazing, brilliant friends would do…I called in backup. LOL! Not just any backup, though. I called in my girls. The brilliant, beautiful, and insanely talented women who I knew could bring this vision to life.

Kaylynn Hunt, E. Raye Turonek, Kenya Moss-Dyme, Keira N. James, Tanisha Stewart, Toni Larue, and Octavia Taneka Grant… and I said, "Y'all, I need you." And because they're the creative powerhouses they are, they said, "Say less."

To each of you…I am so proud of this project. Thank you for trusting me, for jumping into this idea with open hearts and open minds. Your pens are powerful, your hearts are generous, and your talent is unmatched. I'm beyond grateful that you saw my vision and ran with it.

Toni Morrison once said, "If there's a book that you want to read, but it hasn't been written yet, then you must write it."

But when you're blessed with pen sisters who can spin gold out of your imagination… You don't write it alone; you build it together.

So, readers… whether this is your first time meeting these authors or you're already a fan, I present to you Vanished: Six Days in Seven Ways. A bold, multi-layered journey from the creative mind of Ebony Evans, brought to life by seven incredible women I'm honored to call my pen sisters.

Enjoy the ride.

With love,

Introduction

Welcome to Vanished, a groundbreaking collection born from the creative mind of Ebony Evans. Seven authors were recruited to execute. Each author has taken the same narrative and shaped it in their own voice, exploring different possibilities and outcomes that stem from a single starting point. What began as an idea from Ebony Evans has evolved into a journey that allows you, the reader, to experience the same story from multiple perspectives, leading to seven distinct endings.

This experiment in storytelling pushes the boundaries of how we consume narratives, offering you the chance to explore the twists and turns of a tale that is both familiar and ever-changing. As you make your way through each interpretation, you'll see how a single moment can alter the course of destiny in unexpected and captivating ways.

Each ending reflects the author's unique style, voice, and vision. Whether you're drawn to suspense, the romance, the mystery, or the drama, this collection promises to keep you on the edge of your seat until the very last page. So, turn the page and let the adventure unfold—seven times over.

Enjoy the ride.

Acknowledgments

First and foremost, I want to extend my deepest gratitude to Ebony Evans. Your spark of inspiration was the seed that grew into this story, and it wouldn't exist without your brilliant idea. Thank you for sharing your vision, for believing in the potential of this book from the very beginning.

Your creativity lit the path, and I'm so thankful we got to follow it.

To E. Raye, Octavia, Toni, Keira, Tanisha & Kenya, thank you for taking on the challenge. This came together so beautifully. I can't wait to see that orange banner.

~Kaylynn

Vanished

Six Days in Seven Ways

Days 1 - 6

By

Kaylynn Hunt

Day 1

"Dad?"

Layla's voice brought Timothy out of the daydream he was in. He still didn't speak, just looked her way.

"What time did you say you last spoke with your wife?" the officer questioned again.

"Oh." Tim seemed as if he were just recalling where he was. "It was yesterday around 9 o'clock in the morning. She told me she was going to her spa day, then shopping."

"What spa does she go to?"

"Uh..."

"Lovely Touch," Layla interjected.

"Then you stated when you called her again, you got no answer." Tim nodded. "Did you leave a voicemail?"

"No, I thought she might be driving or something. She won't answer while driving, even with the handsfree."

"How long before you called back?"

"I don't know. Maybe an hour. You know, it just dawned on me that she ain't call back nor came in that door. Then when she didn't answer, I called my daughter to see if she was with her."

Tim looked at Layla. "She ain't say you was going with her, but you know sometimes y'all do the mother/daughter thing."

Layla held her father's hand, nodding her head.

"Ms. Merriweather, did you speak with your mother at all yesterday?"

"Yes. It was a little after she talked to Daddy. She told me the same thing. I didn't try to call again until my father called looking for her. There was no answer."

"This is all I need to get the ball rolling. It's important that you try to remain calm. We will keep you up to date with anything we find. And we will surely be in touch if we need anything else from you."

"Thank you, Detective Vernon."

Layla stood then waited for her father to stand and lead the way out of the small office.

"Oh, one more thing. Do you have one of those location tracking accounts for your family?"

"My mom didn't have an app. But she has an iPhone. I tried pinging her location and got nothing. She sometimes turns things on and off on her phone without knowing it. She always complains about stuff being too fancy."

"My mom is the same way," Detective Vernon chuckled while shaking his head. "Like I said, we'll get right on this. I'll be in touch."

"Thank you," Layla responded then continued to the exit.

Layla pulled into her parent's driveway. They hadn't said much to one another the whole way to her parents' home. She knew he was worried about her mother. Asking a lot of questions or trying to get his mind off that would just agitate him. She would be irritated if it were the other way around. So, she kept quiet. Her plan was to now go in this house with him and wait. Make sure he eats, and try to get him to sleep. Maybe she could distract him with soliciting his help with her homework.

Homework made Layla think about school. Was she supposed to go to class tomorrow like nothing was going on? Of course, because there was nothing for her to worry about.

"I know you haven't eaten. Let me get in here and whip you up something," Layla said beelining for the kitchen before Tim could protest.

For the last 25 years, Cherice Merriweather made sure her husband always had a meal. It didn't matter if they had other plans, her cooking was always on deck for him. Even on days she didn't feel like cooking she had a contingency plan. Often when she made large meals, she'd vacuum seal and freeze some for later. That way all she really had to do was warm it up. That's exactly what Layla was about to do.

She placed her laptop on the kitchen counter then found her way to the deep freezer. After riffling around for a bit, she settled on chili. It was simple, quick, and not too much to make her father eat. If he got down a few spoonful it would satisfy her effort. Once she added the chili to a pot, placing it on a low heat on the stove, she sat at the counter.

Tim was in his chair in front of the TV. The news was on, but he wasn't watching it. He was wondering where his wife had gone off to. He stole a glance at Layla as she played around in the kitchen. That girl couldn't cook. He didn't know what she was in there doing, but he wasn't eating it. And why wasn't she distraught? Why didn't he have to comfort her, console her, wipe her tears or hold her hand? The more he thought about it the more he wondered why she wasn't as worried as him.

"Layla," Tim called from his chair.

"Yes, Daddy."

"When you say you talked to your mother last?"

"Yesterday, same as you."

"She ain't call you while she was shopping. I know she always buying you something."

"No, Daddy, she didn't."

Tim grunted; he didn't believe her. Cherice ain't never went too long without calling that girl child of theirs.

"The food is almost done, Daddy."

"I ain't hungry," he said.

"Well, you have to eat something. It's your favorite chili."

"It ain't my favorite if yo' momma didn't make it."

"Daddy, you gone be cantankerous with me today, I see. I bet you $10 it tastes just like Momma's."

"You ain't got $10," he laughed.

"Really, daddy? Come on, if it doesn't taste just like it, you don't have to eat it. But Momma wouldn't want you sitting there starving."

"Fine!"

Tim groaned as he stood from his chair and dragged to the dining table like a child having a tantrum.

"Don't be like that," Layla said as she sat the bowl in front of him. "I want my money too."

She took a seat at the table, picked up her spoon but paused to watch him. He made a show of it as if he had to smell it first. Then he pretended to just taste it with the tip of his tongue. But when he placed the full spoon between his lips and closed his mouth, his eyes lit up. He didn't say anything. That's when Layla took the time to eat what was in front of her. To her pleasure, he'd eaten the entire bowl. When she was done, she got up to clear the dishes.

"I'm going to run home to grab some clothes. I'll stay here with you tonight."

"I don't need no babysitter."

"Maybe I do."

Tim grunted then made his way back to his chair. Layla made sure the dishes were cleaned and in the rack before she headed out. Just as she opened the front door to gather her things she spoke.

"I want my money, Old Man."

Day 2

Layla woke up in what used to be her bedroom. It had since been converted into an office slash guest room with just a day bed. Her mother had insisted on not keeping a teen's room once Layla was gone. After retrieving a few articles of clothing, gathering the rest of her schoolbooks and smoking on a much need blunt, she returned to find her father asleep in his chair.

She didn't dare to wake him; she was glad he was asleep. At least one of them could get some rest. The cool demeanor she'd been sporting was on the notion of being strong for her dad. But on the inside, she was falling apart. And she dared not to let any part of that out for fear she'd never be able to pull it back together.

If she hadn't learned anything else from her mother, she knew how to hide her feelings. She knew how to push them down until she was ready to sulk in them. Cherice and Timothy Merriweather may have been married 25 years but that didn't mean all of them were happy.

Her dad had his moods, she watched Cherice navigate them. There were times when Layla questioned why her mother was still with the man. Not that she didn't love her daddy and not that he ever treated them badly. But there were way too many days it seemed walking on eggshells was something her mom needed to do. Tim could be jealous, insecure, and dependent. It just seemed like a lot to deal with in Layla's opinion.

7

Layla checked the time on her cellphone, it was time for her to get ready for class, if she was going. She still wasn't fully invested in the idea but what else was she to do?

After checking the time turned into scrolling social media, she pulled herself up to go shower. Just as she stepped into the shower, she could've sworn she heard the house phone ringing. Yes, her parents still had a landline phone. Her father refused to get rid of it. But the only people who used it were solicitors. It was too early for that, she must've been mistaken.

"Dad, you want some breakfast before I go to class?"

"No."

Layla took a deep breath. If she hadn't made the decision to go to school, it was a definite now. She wasn't in the mood to navigate his attitude all day.

"I'm headed to school. I'll call to check on you between classes. But if any updates come in, call me."

She kissed her dad on his forehead, he just grunted.

As soon as Layla pulled out of the driveway, their landline phone rang, again. Tim lifted himself from the chair as quickly as he could manage.

It has to be Cherice he thought.

By the time he made it to the phone cradle atop the bureau on the other side of the room, it'd rung three times.

"Hello," he answered with a tone laced with anxiety.

Tim could hear nothing but what sounded like static.

"Cherice, that you? Hello?

The line went dead.

~~~

Layla had been in school trying to concentrate. But more often than not throughout the day, she'd found her mind drifting. Midway into her second class of the day, she decided school may not have been the great idea she thought it would be. Instead of continuing with the rest of her classes, she found a spot in the commons to sit and think.

When Layla returned to her parents' after leaving school, Tim was still in the same spot.

"Dad, did you eat?" she asked standing at the kitchen island after dropping her bookbag there.

"Yeah, I ate some more of your momma's chili."

"Well, you need more than that. And I didn't forget about that money you owe me."

"Um," he grunted.

The phone on the kitchen wall began ringing.

"Hello," Layla answered. "Helloo?"

She replaced the receiver.

"They ain't say nothing, did they?"

"No."

"It's been happening all day."

"Maybe some company's phone system is messed up or something."

"Well, they need to get it fixed. I get excited every time, thinking it might be your momma."

Layla wasn't sure what to say. Reassurance that everything would be fine seemed like a lie because she didn't know if she believed that. She didn't want to discourage him or seem like the hopeless one. But if Layla was nothing else, she was a realist and practical. It was now beyond that 48-hour mark they say is crucial in finding missing people and murderers.

During her time sitting and thinking while on campus, it occurred to her there were some phone calls she should've made. She was beyond worried now. Layla's unbothered resolve was dwindling. Her mother hadn't called her in two days. There wasn't a time in her life she could ever remember that happening.

"I'll be back later, Daddy. I'm going to check on my place."

Layla didn't wait for his response before she was out the door. As soon as she got in her car, she hit the hands-free button on her steering wheel.

"Call Lovely Touch."

"Dialing Lovely Touch," the robotic voice replied as she backed out the driveway.

Layla listened to the ringing coming through her speakers while simultaneously checking the time, making sure it wasn't past closing.

"Lovely Touch, this is Aveda. How may I help you?"

"Hey Aveda. This is Layla Merriweather."

"Hey girl. What's up? You trying to get an appointment?"

"I need one but no, that's not why I'm calling."

"What you need girl?"

"I was wondering if you could tell me what time my mom left the other day."

"Let me see." Aveda was typing on her keyboard, pulling up the records. "Layla, girl, what day are you talking about?"

"Tuesday."

"You sure? I don't see an appointment in here for Ms. Cherice."

"She told us she had a spa day."

"Is everything ok?"

"Aveda, no one has spoken to my mother since Tuesday. A detective hasn't come in to talk to you guys?"

"Not that I know of. Not while I was here. I hope Ms. Cherice is alright. Maybe she went to a different place. She's cheated before."

"What did you say?"

Aveda chuckled.

"I always tease her about cheating on us that one time she tried to go someplace else."

"Oh, yeah." Layla attempted to a fake laugh.

"Layla if you need us to do anything, let me know. I'll keep an eye out."

"Thank you, Aveda."

As the call disconnected, Layla steered her vehicle into the nearest parking lot she saw. Once in a space, she dug through her purse looking for Detective Vernon's phone number.

She sat looking at all the things she discarded from her bag sprawled across her passenger seat as the phone rang.

"Detective Vernon," he answered.

"Detective Vernon, this is Layla Merriweather. I thought you said you were looking for my mother."

"I assure you, Ms. Merriweather, I have been."

"How is that when you haven't even checked with the spa? They ain't seen my momma. She didn't even go there on Tuesday like she said. Why would she lie to me? And you're not doing shit to find her. You said you would handle it. It ain't looking like you're handling shit!"

Layla waited for him to respond, but he said nothing, she checked the phone screen to ensure she was still connected even though she could hear background noise.

"HELLO?"

"I'm here Ms. Merriweather. I was giving you a minute to catch your breath."

Layla didn't respond. If she wasn't so angry, she may have been embarrassed.

"It's understandable that you're frustrated, emotional and worried about your mom. But I assure you, I'm doing my job. I'm aware that your mom didn't go to the spa because I received her location information from her cell phone company. I'd planned to come by to talk with you and your dad in the morning. Can we schedule a good time that I can speak with you both?"

"Can you come at nine?"

"I'll see you then."

"Ok," Layla said before hitting end on her phone.

Day 3

Layla had just put on the coffee when the doorbell rang. She had been up for hours lying in her bed staring at the ceiling. She couldn't stop thinking about the fact that her mother had never even gone to the spa. Where could she have been? What was she doing? AND why did she lie?

When Layla opened the front door, she paused a bit before she greeted the detective. *This man is fine. What is wrong with me? I shouldn't be thinking about how fine he is.*

"Good morning, Detective Vernon. Come on in."

Layla showed him to the living room where her father sat in his chair. She offered him a seat on the adjacent sofa.

"I need to grab my cup of coffee. Would you like a cup?"

"I'm fine, thank you."

Layla returned with a cup for her father then sat on the opposite side of the detective.

"So, what did you find out?" Tim asked.

"Well, Mr. Merriweather, we haven't found your wife yet. I can give you some information but not all as we are still openly investigating. I'd like to ask you a few more questions as well. But let me start with this. We pulled Mrs. Merriweather's phone records. Do either of you recognize this number?"

He handed them a Post-it with a phone number scribed on it. Tim looked at it then passed it to Layla.

"I don't offhand. Let me get my phone," she said before standing. "That's not a number I have in my phone," she continued after searching her contacts.

Layla handed the paper back to the detective.

"We know that Mrs. Merriweather didn't go to the spa as she told both of you. Is there anywhere else she's been known to frequent?"

"Wh..wh…what you mean she didn't go to the spa?"

Detective Vernon gave a quick glance at Layla— her eyes were pleading. She hadn't told her father what she found out and she didn't want him to give away her treachery.

"When we checked her phone's location information it didn't show that she'd been in that area. Which brings me to another point, is there anyone she would possibly visit out of state?"

"Why do you ask that?" Layla questioned.

"It seems that she was at or near the airport before her location reporting was switched off."

Layla's eyes filled with tears. Tim sat up in his chair.

"So, she turned the location off on purpose." Layla said.

It was more of a statement than a question.

"We don't know that yet. All we know is that it stopped reporting. We'll know more when we're able to look at the airport surveillance. As of right now, we cannot issue any Silver Alerts, and we would urge you to not go to the media just yet."

"Because you think she just left us," Layla said softly.

"I'm not saying that Ms. Merriweather. We simply don't know what the situation is at this time."

He wanted to go on to say that maybe someone else had her phone, maybe she'd been kidnapped, maybe she ran off the road, maybe a lot of other things, but nothing he would've said could possibly make them feel better. Detective Vernon could see the pain in Layla's eyes. The anguish etched into her beautiful face almost caused him pain.

Tim hadn't said anything else, he stared at the floor. The detective wasn't only there to give them the information, he was there to observe their reactions.

"I.." *Ring*

Layla's statement was interrupted by the ringing telephone. She immediately crossed the room to retrieve the receiver from the cradle.

"Hello? HelLO? HELLO!"

She hung up then placed her forehead against the wall trying to will the tears that had formed not to fall. To no avail.

"Has that happened before?" The detective questioned.

"Yeah, they called all yesterday. When I picked up, nobody said anything," Mr. Merriweather stated absently.

"Do I have permission to put a trace on your phone? We can find out who's doing this."

"If you think it'll help find my wife, do what you want."

"I'll get right on that. If there's anything else that happens, don't hesitate to call," he said as he stood.

"Let me walk you out."

Layla escorted him to the door, opening it for him then stepping onto their small porch with him.

"Thank you again detective." She extended her hand.

"It's my job. I wish there was more information, but I'm working on it."

"And I wanted to apologize for my call to you yesterday. It was just-"

"Your emotions are high, it's frustrating. I get it. I'm not holding anything against you," Detective Vernon stated.

Layla's face let way to a slight grin as he took her hand.

"You hang in there. We're working to find her."

Detective Vernon released Layla's hand, and she released a breath with a nod. As he retreated from the porch, she watched him to his car before going inside. After closing the door, she turned around to address her father. He wasn't in his chair.

"Daddy?"

He hadn't answered but she could hear some rustling which sounded as if it was coming from upstairs. After climbing the stairs, she found him in the master bedroom. He'd placed a duffle bag on the bed and was frantically moving from the closet throwing things inside.

"Dad. What are you doing?"

"I'm going to the airport."

"What? Where are you going?"

"Wherever your momma went."

"But Daddy we don't know if she was there or not."

"They gone tell me."

Layla took a deep breath. She knew more than anyone how stubborn this man she loved could be.

"Daddy, even if you knew what airline to ask, they won't tell you. And if you go there acting a fool, they will put you on the no-fly list and you won't be able to fly anywhere to get anybody."

"Humph," he grumbled as he flopped on the edge of the bed.

"I know you're worried, Daddy. Let's just wait until the detective can tell us something concrete. If she got on a plane going anywhere, I'll fly with you."

Tim nodded his head then headed back to his chair.

Layla went into her bedroom and closed the door. She paced the floor with her cell phone in her hand. Mentally, she debated with herself. Giving in to the inkling that was tickling the back of her brain, she dialed his number.

"Hello," his baritone voice answered after the third ring.

"Hi, uh, is my mom with you?"

"Layla?"

"Yeah, I'm sorry. How are you?"

"Don't worry about pleasantries, what's happened with Reece?"

Mr. Uncle, that was what Layla called him when she was ten, was an old friend of her mother's. They'd been friends for many years and called themselves liking each other in high school.

Cherice would sometimes have lunch with him, go to the museum, art gallery, all the things Tim had no interest in. At times, Layla went along. That was until her father found out about it. She remembered the big fight they'd had. Ultimately, Tim won, as he always did. Cherice stopped meeting up with Bruce. But Layla knew they still stayed in touch.

In fact, it was just a few months ago that Cherice had passed his number along to her to use as a reference for the internship she wanted to apply for. He was the head of a design firm, an endorsement from him went a long way. He happened to have moved to Illinois. Layla thought that maybe…

"That's just it, we haven't heard from her in three days now. The officer said the last ping they got from her phone was near the airport. I thought…," she let the last of her statement go unsaid.

"Ohhh Lay, I'm so sorry. I haven't talked to Reece in months. Besides she wouldn't leave y'all for me. Believe me I know," he chuckled to ease the bitterness from his statement.

"It was worth a try."

"Listen, if I hear from her, I'll be sure to let you know. But you gotta promise that if you need anything, you let me know. I mean it, anything. And please let me know when you find her."

"I will. Thanks, Mr. Uncle."

He laughed before disconnecting.

Vanished

Layla wasn't sure if she was elated or disappointed.

Day 4

Tim was in motion as soon as Layla left for school. He didn't care what she said, he was heading to the airport. From the time the detective mentioned the airport, he knew where Cherice had gone. He stood at the curb looking at the house for a minute before he made his way up the walkway.

The entire night, he'd sat awake thinking of Cherice with her lover. It had been years since he'd allowed himself to think of her in the arms of another. But Bruce Canton was the bane of his existence. Between the time the detective left and this very moment it had been the only thing on his mind. Their big falling out years prior, played over and over in his head.

He'd overheard Layla and Cherice talking about a day they had at the science center. At first, he thought nothing of it, it was what mothers and daughters did. But when he heard her mention an uncle, he began to wonder who the hell she was talking about. When they got ready to lay down for the night, he questioned her.

"Y'all had a day out, huh?"

"I told you we were going on an outing."

"But who is the uncle Lay was talking about? Last I checked you didn't have a brother."

Cherice sighed heavily. Tim watched her shoulders slump.

"Bruce."

"Bruce, who is that?"

"A friend."

"Cherice, start talking. Where this friend come from? I don't know a fucking Bruce."

"I've known him most of my life. We ran into each other a while ago." She shrugged as if it were no big deal. "He called while we were out, he met us there."

"So, you had some strange man around my daughter?"

"Please Timothy. He isn't a strange man. I just told you I've known him most of my life."

"Wait! Bruce. Your high school sweetheart, Bruce?"

"I wouldn't call us sweethearts."

"Everyone else would. Hell no!"

"What do you mean, Hell no?"

"I mean. Hell no, you can't see him."

"You're being ridiculous."

"I'm being your husband. It's him or us."

She left him. Layla was gone and she'd finally did it, left him. There was no convincing him that his wife hadn't left him for her true love. Bruce did the things she liked, he took care of himself, he would take care of her. Bruce had more money, more charisma, and more personality. So, as he now stood prepared to knock on the door of the man that took his wife, he was resolved that he was getting her back.

Knock, knock, knock....

When the door swung open, Tim was surprised to see a petite woman. She put him in the mind of Cherice. They were about the same height, long hair like Cherice, the woman had a little more hip and her complexion was much darker. But still it was something about her that seemed like his wife.

"May I help you?"

"I-I-I was looking for Cherice."

"I'm sorry sir. I don't know a Cherice."

"Is Bruce here?"

"Yes. One moment." She closed the door. "Honey," Tim heard her call.

When Bruce pulled the door open, he was surprised to see Tim standing there. He stepped out closing the door behind him.

"Tim? What are you doing here?"

"I was looking for my wife. Have you seen her?"

"No, I haven't seen her since the day you showed up at my job telling me to stay away from her."

Flashes of the day replayed in Bruce's head, it made him angry. But he tempered his anger, he knew why he was there. Though he would never let on that Layla had called him.

"Have you spoken to her?"

"I haven't. I don't know what this is about, why you're at my house or how you even know where I live. But I don't appreciate you showing up here."

"We ain't seen Cherice in four days now. If you talk to her, just let her know we're looking for her. Apologies showing up out the blue."

Tim nodded his head and started back toward the street.

"I hope everything is ok. I'm sure she'll come home soon," Bruce called out to him.

Tim looked back, nodded his head then climbed into the car he'd rented and headed back to the airport.

~~~

Layla had every intention of going to school and pretending to be present the same way she'd been doing all week. It was another day down with no real answers, no clues, no mom. But instead of pulling into the parking lot of her college campus, she found herself pulling into the driveway of her own home. The home she hadn't slept in since all this started.

"What the hell?" she questioned out loud.

There was a car parked in her driveway. Her eyes rolled to the back of her head, and she blew out an exasperated breath. After grabbing her bag from the passenger's seat, she opened the door to step out of the car. Before she could stand to her full height, he'd climbed out of his and was leaning against it waiting for her to pass.

"What are you doing here, Langston?"

"You haven't answered my calls or texts."

"That's because I don't want to talk to you."

"Where have you been?"

"None of your fucking business."

Layla stormed past him wishing he would just go away. Even though she knew, she probably wouldn't be so lucky.

"Layla, please. Just let me explain."

"There is nothing to explain, Langston. We ran our course. I'm not even mad at you for seeking out someone else. We haven't been aligned lately. It's ok. Just leave me alone."

"It wasn't like that."

"So, I didn't see you kissing Beatrice Gamble?"

"You did but.."

"But-it's cool. I really haven't had a second thought about it. I have other things on my mind.

And in all honesty, she hadn't. It was just before her father called inquiring about her mother that Layla walked out of the bookstore when she walked right into Langston and Beatrice's lip lock. Of course, Langston hadn't expected to run into her. They weren't anywhere near school or home. She'd just so happened to go to the little suburb looking for a rare book. Ironically, it was for him.

They had fallen into a lull lately. The book was her way of trying to demonstrate some thoughtfulness, caring, and appreciation. After all, it had been a tough year for them both. Classes had been demanding, more so than either of them realized. Layla thought of the book as a declaration that she was still in it. And obviously, he wasn't.

"Layla, she kissed me. It wasn't like that at all. We'd gone for lunch; she told me she needed help with her chem lab. She pressed her lips to mine."

"And you didn't stop her, you didn't pull away. You just let her."

Ring... Ring... Ring...

Layla's ringing phone interrupted.

"Hello."

"Lay?"

"You heard from Momma?"

"No, honey I haven't but your father just paid me a visit."

"What?!"

"He came looking for Cherice."

"I can't believe him."

"I can. He is lost. The love of his life is gone. I guess he thought she was here with me.

"What did you tell him? Where is he now?"

"I told him what I told you. I haven't spoken with her in months. I'm not sure where he is now. He left a few minutes ago. I just wanted you to know where he was and not worry you with two missing parents."

"Thank you, Mr. Uncle."

"No problem. Like I said, if you need anything from me, don't hesitate to ask."

"I won't."

They disconnected without another word. Layla's thoughts were churning a mile a minute. When Langston began speaking again, it pulled her thought back to the present.

"I was in shock. I really didn't know what to do. And when I saw you, my heart broke."

"Ha! That makes two of us."

"I told your mom it was a big misunderstanding."

"What do you mean you told my mom?"

"You ran off, weren't answering your phone. So, I called her."

"She answered?"

"Yeah, at first, I thought she might not, knowing you'd probably told her what happened."

"What did she say?"

"She told me to just explain it to you. But she told me to give you a day or two to calm down. We laughed about how you don't hear anything when you're angry."

"What time was that?"

He shrugged. "Maybe around noon, one o'clock."

"How did she sound?"

"What do you mean? She sounded like herself. Maybe a little distracted, I think she was having lunch with someone."

"Did she say where she was?"

"No. Wait. Why are you asking me all this? What's going on Layla?"

"It seems, you're the last one to speak to my mother before she disappeared.

Day 5

Unlike the previous days, Layla woke up with a plan. Speaking with Langston helped to ground her thoughts. That was one thing about the two of them, they balanced one another. After speaking with him, relaying the information to Detective Vernon and filling Langston in on the events of the previous days, her mind seemed clearer. There were things she hadn't thought of things she could've done.

Calling around to hospitals was number one on the list. Why she hadn't thought of that before, she didn't know. Perhaps it was because she was letting the police handle it. But even more, she wasn't ready to think of that. Langston was a big help. After he learned what she had been going through, he refused to leave her side. She still hadn't taken the time to decide if she believed his version of events yet, but she appreciated his gesture.

They sat across from one another at her dining room table going down a list of hospitals in the area. They checked each one off as they went down the list. Again, stuck between relief and despair, Layla didn't know what to do when they got to the bottom of the list. There were still no answers.

"You do?"

Layla perked up when she heard Langston's response. Maybe he'd found her. She'd begun to get excited however,

Langston's face didn't have a hint of glee. She watched as he listened intently to the person on the other end. Impatiently, she peered at the list to try to garner which facility he was speaking with. But they'd already checked off everyone.

"And what are those hours?" Langston continued speaking on the phone. "Thank you. We'll see you soon."

"Yes! You found her? Where?"

Layla hopped from her seat, and began gathering her things, she was ready to head out. Then she noticed that Langston hadn't moved. And the expression on his face was somber.

"What are you waiting for? Let's go. What hospital?"

"Lay, we're not sure if it's her. They said they had a Jane Doe about your mother's age."

"Ok. Let's go!"

"But Layla, I—"

"You what? Come on," she interrupted.

"Take a second."

"I'll take a second in the car. Let's go," she said as she now stood at the door with her hand on the knob to open it.

Layla wasn't trying to hear anything Langston had to say. All she wanted to know was what hospital she would be pulling up at. While he was so desperately trying to find the words to say what else he had to say. When Layla snatched the door open, he had to rein her in.

"Layla!" He yelled to get her attention. "That wasn't a hospital, it was the morgue."

~~~

Tim pushed into his front door, greeted by the ringing phone. He snatched the handheld from its cradle after crossing the floor in record time.

"Hello." He was met with a bit of static but no voice. "Who is this?" Still there was no answer. "What do you want? Stop calling here!" he said before hanging the phone up.

After being at the airport all night, he wasn't in the mood to play on the phone. He called Layla and told her not to come back last night and that he needed to be alone. The shame and embarrassment he felt wouldn't allow him to tell her the truth. She hadn't fought him about it. It shocked him, he just knew she'd give him more push back. But maybe she was sick of him too.

Once he shed his clothes and took a much-needed shower, Tim was resolved to get in his chair. He needed to find something on the television to distract his thoughts. He'd spent all night trying to think of where else Cherice could've been or even why she would've left. There wasn't anything they'd fought about recently, nothing she'd complained that he'd done or hadn't. He was at a loss.

It was nearly a week with no word from her. The hopefulness Tim tried to hold on to was dwindling. If she'd gone because of him, he could get her back. That's what he thought anyway. If he'd made her mad, he could fix it. But if, just if something had happened to her, he didn't know what he would do, how he would survive, what kind of life would he have.

Ding....Dong....

The doorbell pulled Tim from his thoughts. His head whipped towards the door. His mind bounced between who could it be and the fact that he was too tired to get up. Pushing himself up from the chair he ambled to the door. When he looked out the peephole, no one was there.

Tim snatched the door open, there was a small package on the stoop in front of the door.

"What the hell?"

He stepped out onto the porch craning his next looking up, down and across the street. There was no one in sight then he tried to recall if he'd heard a vehicle pull away. Once he picked up the package, he carried it into the house then sat it on the kitchen counter.

"This must be something Cherice ordered," he told himself then began to walk back to his chair.

Before getting back in his chair, he decided to back track to the kitchen to grab a drink and make himself a sandwich.

Tim had his triple decker sandwich, a side of potato chips and his big plastic cup full of Kool-Aid ready to sit in front of the TV and pretend for just a little while that nothing was wrong in his life. His wife was just at the store, his daughter was at school, and he was getting some quiet time to himself. That's what he chose for his mindset, that's where he wanted his focus. Not anything that was reality at that moment. That notion was short lived.

When he rounded the kitchen counter all his aspirations were doused as he slipped. The sandwich tumbled to the floor along with the cup in his hand as he successfully stopped himself from falling when he grabbed the edge of the counter. Tim took a minute to calm his heart and breathing.

"Would that just be the cherry on the cake," he said to himself. "Well, there goes my sandwich."

As he bent to pick up the scattered remnants of his lunch, he noticed the sandwich lying in the Kool-Aid. Tim began shaking his head looking at the mess he made. After throwing the sandwich in the garbage and the cup in the sink, he fished the mop out of the broom closet. Taking the dry mop, he began soaking up the spilled liquid but all it did was smear across the floor.

"What the hell is this?"

Tim then noticed what he thought was Kool-Aid seemed darker and thicker than the cherry beverage previously in his cup. Taking in the scene all at once, actually paying attention to what was in front of him, he noticed the trail that seeped from the package he'd set on the counter.

Tim gasped! *Is that blood?*

~~~

Layla stood nestled in Langston's arms in the lobby of the morgue. She'd just given them her information and was waiting for them to do whatever they needed to do for her to identify the body. When her cell phone rang, she was just about to answer her father's call when she thought better of it. She then decided instead to send him to voicemail until she figured out what was going on.

What would she tell him? That she was about to identify her mother's body, and she couldn't talk to him right at that moment or would she lie and say she was at the movies or something. Her mind then jumped to how she would have to tell him if this were in fact her mother laying back there unidentified. She was just about to answer when the second round of rings revealed Tim calling her back when the attendant opened the door.

"You can come this way."

She quickly tucked her cell into her pocket then followed the employee through the doors down the stark white hall. They stopped in front of a window that put her in the mind of an observation room of some sort. The window was covered by a drawn curtain on the other side.

"Wait here, they'll pull the curtain in a few seconds, you will be able to view the body."

Layla took a deep breath, willing herself to calm down. It was useless though. As soon as the curtain began to move her heart rate increased. Langston held her hand, squeezing as tightly as he could without hurting her.

"OMG!" Layla exclaimed once the body was in full view.

Then she fainted.

~~~

Detective Vernon made it to the Merriweather's home in record time. He'd used his siren up until he was two blocks away. He didn't want to bring more attention to their home than necessary. The crime scene van would soon be in front of the house. There would already be plenty for the neighbors to gossip about, the sirens would just make things worse.

When he arrived, Tim Merriweather was sitting on the front step with a beer in his hand. The look on his face was of relief when he recognized the detective. He stood immediately, meeting the detective in the middle of the walkway.

"Mr. Merriweather," he greeted.

"Detective."

"So, you say this package was delivered."

"I didn't see who left it. They rang the bell, and by the time I got to the door they were gone. I thought it was some package Cherice ordered. It was just sitting up on the counter."

Detective Vernon looked around, noting that one of the neighbors across the street had a ring camera. He wondered if it had caught anything.

"Show me the package."

Tim headed towards the front door with the detective close behind. Once inside, he pointed him in the direction of the package but stayed near the door.

"What happened here?" Detective Vernon inquired looking at the mop and blood smears on the floor.

"I-I-I thought it was Kool-Aid I spilled at first. I was trying to clean it up. When I realized what it was, I called you right away. I been sitting outside ever since."

"Where's your daughter?"

"I don't know. I tried to call her when I was waiting for you, but she didn't answer. She probably in class, got an exam or something."

"I'm going to open this," the detective said while putting on the gloves he pulled from his pocket.

Tim nodded then realized the detective wasn't looking at him.

"Yes, sir."

Detective Vernon pulled a small pocketknife from his pants and cut the tape that held the box closed. He slowly pulled up the flap while making sure there was no kind of wire or anything. It was at that moment he thought that maybe he should've had to bomb squad come examine it as well. Once he'd successfully gotten all four flaps open, he peered inside.

Tim watched as the detective's eyes grew wide and jaw tightened. Their eyes met when he looked in Tim's direction. His face was somber.

"Oh no!" Tim exclaimed just before everything went black.

Day 6

The Replacement – By: Kaylynn Hunt

Kaylynn, a Detroit native and multi-genre author, passionately inspires others to follow their dreams, proving it's never too late to pursue one's passions. Residing in the Metropolitan Detroit area, she finds joy in reading, spending time with family and friends, and collaborating with fellow authors to create stories that challenge conventions and spark fresh perspectives. Her imaginative works draw from personal experiences, weaving narratives that encourage readers to think beyond the ordinary. With a commitment to originality, Kaylynn stands as a beacon of creativity and self-expression, fostering growth and inviting others to embrace the extraordinary.

Layla and Tim sat across from detective Vernon with their hands wound together. They were each using one another to hold on to hope. Following the ending of their last day, they both had a new perspective on how things could turn out. They'd both ended up in the same emergency room after passing out. The doctors had concluded in each case it was stress and anxiety that caused them to black out.

Tim had felt like a fool once he was informed there was some sort of scented oil that Cherice had in fact ordered whose bottle had broken in that package. Layla was both relieved and sad to see the woman lying on the slab was not her mother. But they'd both come to the conclusion that they'd been in denial of the fact that this situation may end gravely.

Detective Vernon called early this morning asking them to come to the station.

Layla had managed to convince Langston that he shouldn't accompany her to the station. She knew she should feel grateful that he'd been around to support her. But instead, she was beginning to feel like she was suffocating. He hadn't given her a minute to herself. She was still churning over all the things that had transpired in the last few days. There had to be something she was missing.

"Mr. & Ms. Merriweather, I won't draw this out. I just wanted to update you. Based on the information we received from your boyfriend."

"Ex-boyfriend," Layla cut in.

"With the timeline Mr. Langston Miles provided, we were able to track down where she was at lunch. I'd like you to look at this photo, tell me if you know this person."

Detective Vernon handed the photocopied photo to Layla. Cherice stood at the counter with a woman she had never seen before. The woman resembled her mother in some ways, her eyes, the way they stood. Though the photo was not in full color or even a clear picture there was something familiar about her. When she passed the photo to Tim, he stiffened.

If this had been earlier in the week, Tim would've told the detective unequivocally that he didn't know that woman. But this wasn't day one —it was day six since he'd last seen his wife. He met this woman on day four. She was the woman at Bruce's house. The one he thought was Cherice at first. The woman that looked at him as if she had no clue who he was, but she must've. She was with his wife.

Detective Vernon noticed Mr. Merriweather's body language. He studied the change in his facial expressions before speaking.

"Mr. Merriweather, you know this woman?"

"I don't know her, but I've seen her."

Layla's head whipped in her father's direction.

"Where Daddy,? When did you see this woman?"

Tim was hesitant to answer. He was embarrassed to admit it to his daughter or anyone for that matter, out loud.

"She was at Bruce Canton's home. I went there looking for Cherice two days ago."

He held his chin high, refusing to let his gaze go to the floor like his conscience urged him to. Layla looked at the side of his face while he stared into Detective Vernon's eyes.

"Who is Bruce Canton?"

"He's an old friend of my mother's."

"He's my wife's ex-lover," Tim stated pointedly.

Layla took in a sharp breath. She'd always thought of her father as jealous and possessive but what if he was right?

"What happened when you went there? Where does Mr. Canton live?"

"He lives in Ohio. When you said Cherice was near the airport, I thought she may have gone to him. He assured me he hadn't seen her. But this woman answered his door."

Tim leaned forward dropping the photocopy on the detective's desk.

"You should've shared this with me." Detective Vernon began typing on his computer. "Do you have a contact number for him?"

"No," Tim responded.

"I do."

It was Tim's turn to whip his head in his daughter's direction, she didn't look his way. Explaining how or why she had Mr. Uncle's number wasn't on her list of things to do in this moment. She rattled off the digits to the detective.

Detective Vernon didn't bother to usher them from his office, he dialed the number.

"Hello, Mr. Canton?"

"Yes?"

"This is Detective Vernon from the Detroit Police department. I'd like to ask you a few questions about Cherice Merriweather."

"I'm not sure I can help detective. I've let both Layla and Tim know that I haven't seen Cherice."

"I understand that but there has been some new information that's come to light."

"Mr. Merriweather says there was a woman at your home when he visited."

"Yes, my friend, Ramona."

"Is she with you now?"

"No, why?"

"We have reason to believe she's seen Mrs. Merriweather recently."

"I don't understand how that could be. They've never met to my knowledge."

"What's the nature of your relationship with Ramona. What's her last name?"

"Coleman. And we're friends, it's complicated."

"I'm sending you a picture of a picture, tell me if this is Ramona."

{ding...ding} Bruce pulled his cell from his ear to look at the photo that'd just come through.

"This does look like Ramona. I don't understand what's going on."

"Mr. Canton, I've got an idea. Can you call Ms. Coleman and conference me in. I'm going to remain quiet. I just want you to find out where she is right now."

"Ok. I can do that."

"Give me one second though. First, can you give me her cell number?" Detective Vernon jotted down the number Bruce rattled off then continued. Let me get a few things set up here before you call. I'm going to place you on hold.

"Ok.

Detective Vernon muted his phone but placed it on speaker while he picked up his desk phone to call the tech. He ordered a trace on Ramona's number. After unmuting the call, he continued with the call on speaker but not before placing a finger to his lips for the Merriweather's silence.

"You can proceed Mr. Canton, try to keep her on the line at least 3 minutes."

"That shouldn't be a problem," Bruce said before placing the detective on hold, placing the call and conferencing him in.

Detective Vernon placed his phone on mute as he and the Merriweathers listened in.

"Hey!" Ramona greeted.

"Hey, what are you up to?"

"Headed to pick up groceries for dinner tonight."

"That's right you're cooking me dinner tonight."

"Don't tell me you forgot."

"I didn't forget completely just realizing tonight is the night I guess," he chuckled.

"It sure is. I'm going to make you the best meal you've ever had."

"What time should I be over?"

"Oh, no. I'm cooking over there."

"You don't have to do that. It seems like a lot to have you bring groceries here."

"It's no bother."

"Well, what time will you be over?"

"Around six if that's fine."

"Sure. That's fine. I'm working from home today, I'll be here."

"Any word on your friend?"

"Cherice? No, not that I know of."

"I hope they find her. It's got to be so awful for her family."

"Yeah, me too," Bruce said somberly.

"I know you're worried for her too."

"We've known each other a long time. I would hate for something to happen to her. Her daughter would be devastated."

"So would you."

"Sure, but I'm more worried for her family." Bruce couldn't help but think that her statements were a little puzzling.

"Well, honey. I'm pulling up at the store now. I'll see you about six."

"Ok, enjoy your shopping. See you this evening." After Bruce made sure the call was disconnected, he spoke again. "Was that good enough?"

"You did very well, Bruce."

"I'm not too sure about that conversation. She's never really asked about Cherice before; it was kind of strange."

"I'm going to check into some things on this end. I'll be giving you a call back in a few. Plan on keeping that dinner date. I'm going to be in touch."

"I'll be waiting by the phone."

Once they disconnected, he looked at the Merriweathers.

"I know it's going to be hard, but you guys go home. There's a lot of things to be done here and in Ohio. I'll give you an update as soon as I have one."

Tim nodded as did Layla, they stood, got in Tim's car, and headed in the direction of home.

~~~

By the time Detective Vernon's feet touched the helipad at the airport in Ohio, he'd worked out a plan with Bruce. The detective he'd been in touch with met him as he got out the chopper.

"Detective Vernon, Whorton," the local detective stated as he reached out his hand.

"Hello. Thanks for your assistance," Detective Vernon greeted while joining in the handshake.

"No problem. We've managed to get a search warrant for the home of Ms. Coleman. I have two unmarked vehicles on Mr. Canton's block."

"Let's head out."

Once they got into the awaiting vehicle, Whorton filled him in on what they'd found out about Ms. Coleman. Detective Vernon gave his account of what he thought might be going on. They arrived at Ramona's home. Vernon noticed the video doorbell as soon as they stepped close to the front door. They knocked on the door even with the bell there. Vernon opted to push the door chime also even though it had probably already alerted Ramona of their presence.

~~~

Ramona was preparing the meal she had planned for Bruce, there was music playing and they laughed and talked as she cooked. Bruce kept reminding himself not to keep checking the time. He wanted to watch his phone for missed calls. But he didn't want Ramona to get suspicious. He'd heard her phone vibrate in her purse, but she didn't bother to check it.

"I got us some wine," Bruce said as he sat a full wine glass on the counter.

"Thank you. You got my favorite."

"It's the least I could do for this meal."

There was more small talk until Ramona placed what she needed into the oven. As they waited for the meal to cook, Ramona finally fished her phone out of her purse to check it.

"Is everything ok?"

The look on Ramona's face was full of fright.

"Yes, yes, just the package I'd been waiting on was delivered. I can grab it later."

They moved into the den to the awaiting program on the television. Bruce observed Ramona's demeanor, she seemed restless.

~~~

"There's nothing here. No sign of Mrs. Merriweather," Whorton stated.

"It's time for a chat with Ramona Coleman." {Buzz…. Buzz} "Vernon," he answered his ringing cellphone. "What?! I'm on my way."

"What was that about?" Whorton questioned once he disconnected the call.

"We gotta get over to Bruce Canton's house."

~~~

"Do you want me to go grab your package?"

"Huh?" Ramona questioned.

"You seem to be worried about the package you were waiting for. Do you want me to go get it for you. You're only about fifteen minutes away," Bruce explained.

"Oh, no. You don't have to worry about that. It's nothing. Dinner is almost done," she said dismissively as she went into the kitchen to check the oven.

Just as Ramona placed the roasting pan onto the top of the stove, the doorbell rang. She looked across the room as Bruce got up to head to the door to see who it was then continued what she was doing.

Bruce looked out the cutout in the door and was thrown completely off guard.

"Layla, what are you doing here?" Before she could respond her father stepped into view. "Tim. What's going on here?"

"We need to speak with you. Is it alright if we come in?" Layla questioned but she wasn't really asking, she was already stepping inside.

"I'm about to sit down for dinner with my friend. What can I do for you?"

"It's your **friend** we have a problem with."

"Y'all shouldn't be here," he said trying to usher them back out the door.

"Naw, we're here for answers and we aim to get them," Tim pushed past Bruce.

Tim didn't know where he was going but he smelled food cooking. He bet if he followed his nose he'd find Ramona. Layla looked at Mr. Uncle with a semi-apologetic gaze as she followed behind her father. Bruce hurried after her, trying to get ahead of both of them.

"You can't just come in here."

"Where the hell is she?" Tim asked.

"I don't know," Bruce responded with a confused look on his face. "She was just in here. You all shouldn't be here anyway. Let the police handle this."

"It's been enough days," Tim said with finality.

{Vroom} All their heads turned when they heard what sounded like a car starting up. They darted towards the front door, Layla in the lead. She was faster than both the older gentlemen. But by the time she'd bounded from the door and headed to the street, Ramona was in her car and driving by. Layla had managed to reach the car and was just getting in the driver's seat, all while trying to keep her eyes on the vehicle Ramona was in.

Just as her father got to the passenger's side, she pressed the start button on the car. But before they could pull off, there was what anyone could call a movie scene at the end of the block. Tire screeches and yelling could be heard from where they were halfway down the block. Tim watched as officers pointed their weapons at the vehicle, yelling at Ramona to turn off the vehicle.

Layla wasn't sure what to do as she watched through the windshield. She was resolved to stay put, having enough sense not to get caught in the crossfire. Tim stood just inside the ajar door while Bruce watched from the sidewalk with his mouth agape.

Once Ramona exited the vehicle, she was told to lay on the ground then ultimately cuffed then escorted to one of the officer's cruisers, they began to search the car. Layla, her father and Bruce all waited to see what was next. More vehicles had arrived. Layla could make out Detective Vernon from the distance. That's when she climbed from the vehicle and began to walk to the end of the block slowly.

Detective Vernon approached the car putting on a pair of gloves. There was one officer going through the paperwork in the glove compartment, another was looking through Ms. Coleman's phone, there was another officer searching the back seat for any clues or evidence.

"Pop the trunk," he said to the officer on the driver's side as he passed him.

He stood at the back of the vehicle praying something inside would give him a clue as to where Mrs. Cherice Merriweather was. But when the trunk popped open, he got the shock of his life.

~~~

Layla sat on one side while her father sat on the other. Cherice had drifted off to sleep again. She was dehydrated according to the doctors and still feeling the effects of whatever drug Ramona had given her. The doctors were still waiting to get the results of the tox screen. For now, all she'd been given was an IV to avoid any problems with drug interactions. She had a few scrapes and bruises but for the most part she was ok.

As soon as Layla noticed Detective Vernon waving his hands once he opened the trunk, she took off running. And she nearly collapsed when she reached him. Cherice was in the fetal position and still. She screamed as the detective wrapped his arms around her to stop her from diving in the trunk as well.

"She's breathing, Layla. It's ok. She's breathing."

Layla had heard him, but it didn't stop her screams. It only changed their purpose. There wasn't agony but joy. An emergency vehicle arrived before Layla could gather her composure. Tim had climbed in the ambulance before they could even get Cherice in it. There was no way he was letting her out of his sight. He hadn't left her side since.

"How is she doing?" Detective Vernon asked as he stepped behind the curtain.

Cherice was still in the emergency department, there was one officer standing guard. Vernon had ordered it just as a precaution. They still needed to get all the facts behind all this.

"They say she's dehydrated but she's ok. I can't thank you enough," Layla responded.

"I was just doing my job. But it looks like you two were trying to do my job too."

Tim looked the man squarely in the eyes. In no uncertain terms he was letting the detective know, he didn't care what he had to say. There was no way he wasn't going to get his wife. Once Detective Vernon nodded his understanding, Tim looked back to the Television on the wall which was nothing more than white noise at this point.

"Did you get any information from that Bit..- Woman?"

"We did."

"Why did she do this?"

"To make a long story short, she felt it was because of Cherice that she wasn't getting anywhere with Mr. Canton."

"But my mother hasn't been seeing that man, has she?"

Tim looked up at Vernon to see the answer for himself. Not that it mattered, he wouldn't care if she had. If there was nothing else he was sure of after all this it was that he'd taken for granted his life and his wife. He wasn't going to anymore.

"Not according to Mr. Canton."

"Then what would hurting my mother do for her?"

"I'm not sure she worked all that out fully. But in her mind, your mother was an obstacle that needed moving. And perhaps she was planning on using this 'crisis' to get closer to him. She requested a lawyer before we could get anything else out of her."

"The bitch is crazy, that's what it was," Cherice spoke up groggily. She was bombarded with hugs and kisses. "I'm alright you two. Who is this handsome man that rescued me?"

"Hello, Mrs. Merriweather. I'm Detective Vernon. These two have been looking for you, I was just there to help."

"I'm glad y'all found me."

"If you're up to it, I'd like to ask you some questions."

"You can't wait on that?" Tim questioned.

"It's fine, Tim."

"You need to rest."

"I been sleep for … how many days has it been?"

"SIX!" They all said in unison.

"Shit!"

"Can you tell me how you ended up with Ms. Coleman to begin with?"

"She called me to say she wanted to throw Bruce a party for his birthday in a few months and she wanted my help. I didn't think anything of it. I told my family I was doing something else because well, Bruce is a touchy subject with my husband." She looked his way but then back to Detective Vernon. "We met for lunch, and I didn't think anything was wrong. We talked about the things he liked, what type of music, the theme, who to invite, etc. She walked me to my car and the next thing I knew; I woke up in her garage. She kept going on and on about how I was in the way. I kept telling the bitch, she called me. I hadn't talked to Bruce except a little bit ago when I called to ask him to help Layla with her internship. But other than that, we hadn't really spoken. She had it in her head I was the problem."

"Because he's in love with you," Tim grumbled.

"I'll need you to come make an official statement once you feel up to it," Detective Vernon stated cutting the tension.

Cherice nodded.

"I'll see myself out," Vernon said before turning on his heels.

"Detective," Layla called.

Detective Vernon turned to see Layla coming his way.

"What can I do for you Ms. Merriweather?"

"I just wanted to thank you again AND apologize to you."

"There's no apology needed."

"Yes, there is. I haven't been the most pleasant to you and I know I came off like I didn't think you were doing your job. But you took it all in stride and I appreciate that."

"You were worried about your mother."

"That's no excuse for being a bitch."

"Uh, if there were ever an excuse, that might be the one."

They chuckled.

"Uh, this might be inappropriate and probably a bit insane buuuuuut, can I take you out?"

"I.."

"That is if you're available, I mean, are you married?"

"I.."

"I'm sorry, this is crazy forget I said anything," she rushed out before turning on her heels.

Detective Vernon grabbed her elbow before she could get away. She spun back to him on the same heels.

"First, you have to call me Larry. I'm not married or involved with anyone. But no, you can't take me out."

"Oh, ok. That's fine. Thanks again for helping me get my mom back."

"BUT!" He interrupted. "I'd be happy to take you on a date," he finished with her hand now in his.

Layla allowed a smile to paint her face, her eyes brightened.

"Well, that sounds even better."

Detective Vernon flashed his pearly whites her way.

"I'll call you in a few days."

"You do that."

He began to back away, not wanting to take his eyes off Layla.

"Maybe, there'll be a good thing to come out of all this after all."

"Maybe."

The End....

Or is it?

Husband Material – By: E. Raye Turonek

E. Raye Turonek is a married mother of five. The Detroit, Michigan native resides with her husband and family in a small rural town in Michigan. Since releasing her debut literary work, Compelled to Murder, in 2016 the author has penned five additional novels and also publishes a monthly newsletter highlighting all things literary—as well as astrology forecasts. This multifaced author is looking to fulfill the reader's need for a sensational experience that won't be forgotten.

"What the –," before Detective Vernon could even finish his statement, he'd unholstered his gun. Hard incessant knocks at the side door startled the already spooked duo, escalating their anxiety.

A tall, pale, goofy-looking older gentleman tried peeking inside. "Hey, neighbor."

Tim stood, still in shock at what they uncovered in the leaking package. The detective holstered his weapon then proceeded to open the door. The nosey neighbor began shedding light on their current dilemma the moment the door opened. "Looks like the power is going to be out for a couple of hours. We've got a busted transformer at the end of the block. The electric company is working on it, but they said it could be up to four hours without power. I've got candles and flashlights if you need any. It'll be dark by the time they get the power back on.

"I'm sorry, I didn't get your name."

"I'm George. I live next door." In the midst of his rant, he glanced down at the blood on the detective's hands, then Tim's pants and shoes. George's mouth sat gaped until his eyes darted to the leaking package on the table. "Hey, my wife has been waiting for that package. Looks like the post office busted it up per usual. On top of that they delivered it to the wrong house."

"Well then, looks like you and your wife have some explaining to do." The detective pulled back his suit jacket revealing his badge.

"Oh no, no need to get up in arms. My wife Jenny, she's a makeup and costume artist. The film she's working on is a horror." He tilted his head forward toward the box. "Hence the severed hand..."

Simultaneously, Tim and the detective breathed a sigh of relief. It wasn't Cherice's severed hand that inhabited the mystery box. Still, the question remained, where was she?

At the morgue, Langston knelt beside Layla who remained unresponsive to the light taps and nudges meant to awaken her. He was determined not to leave her side. Layla had been completely unreasonable the day he'd run into her at the bookstore. Langston felt that reasoning with her mother was the only way to get through to her. The events of that fateful day played out in his mind as the mortician rushed over to assist.

Langston recalled chasing her down to discuss his broken relationship with her daughter.

"How are you, Mrs. Merriweather?"

"Well, hello Langston, I'm doing just fine. How are you?"

"Not too good. I was wondering if I could talk to you about Layla?"

She raised her hand, halting what she presumed would be a sorry ass excuse. They always had one, she thought. "Listen Langston, I don't want to get in the middle of what you and Layla have going on. I don't even know you like that. Certainly not well enough to go against what my daughter deems as best for herself. We raised her right. She knows exactly how a man should and shouldn't be treating her."

"I understand. I do. But please, just hear me out. Can I buy you a coffee? Maybe we can chat over lunch."

"Now, lunch is a little harder for me to turn down. I am famished."

"Great," Langston exclaimed before she could change her mind. "There's a great brunch spot that just opened up in Midtown, Pass A Plate Café. Have you dined there before?"

"I haven't but I had planned to."

"My truck is right over there. I'll drive. That way I'm not taking up your time and gas..."

"Sounds good to me," Cherice remarked.

Langston allowed Cherice to wrap her arm around his as they strolled to his vehicle. Wanting to make the best impression possible he opened her door then helped her inside.

"Thank you, young man," she cooed yet quickly reminded herself of his transgressions against her daughter. Don't let him get one over on you, Cherice. You already know the overlay for the underplay, she thought.

"So, what kind of music do you like to listen to?" Langston inquired.

"I prefer jazz piano music. It relaxes me."

Upon her admission Langston fiddled with the dial on the radio to find an XM station that broadcast Cherice's musical preference. "Is this good?" he asked having stumbled upon a smooth jazz station.

"It's perfect, thank you."

"No problem."

"You seem like such a nice young man. It's a shame you and Layla didn't work out."

Her statement hit Langston like a ton of bricks. His stomach felt as if it were in knots. He wanted to tell her that it wasn't over. Not by a long shot... But decided against it. Keeping calm and making nice would be his best bet. "Well, I certainly plan to do everything I can to prove to Layla that she's mistaken about me."

Cherice huffed. "Good luck with that. She's one tough cookie."

"Yes, I'm aware. She's very stubborn."

"I wouldn't say stubborn. My baby just knows her worth. And it seems to me that now, you do as well..."

"I always knew. Trust me, this is just one big misunderstanding."

"It's not my trust you require, son."

Langston sighed, realizing the truth in her reply. "I was kinda hoping that if I proved to you that I'm a good man, worthy of your daughter you could put in a good word for me. You know… talk to her about giving me another chance."

"Listen son, I understand where you're coming from but as I told you, I don't involve myself in my daughter's affairs. Besides, chatting through lunch is certainly not enough time to judge your character accurately. You want me to play Russian Roulette with my daughter's heart." Cherice shook her head adamantly, "No, sir."

Langston tightened his grip on the steering wheel with both hands. His agitation had reached its peak. There was no way he was giving up on Layla. Convincing her mother would be the only way; he'd assumed her father would pick up on his fuckboy energy immediately. Just then, Langston made a hard right turn. Cherice noticed that the direction in which he was headed was opposite from Midtown but refrained from panicking. She felt remaining calm gave her more of an advantage. Keeping her cellphone hidden at her side she sent out a text. "I have to admit, I am interested in what you have to say."

Langston didn't say another word. At least not until he neared his destination. Once he pulled into a lot housing an abandoned building she finally asked, "Why are we here? This building is abandoned."

"I figured we needed someplace to talk privately," Langston uttered in a monotone voice.

"But…." Cherice attempted to rebuttal but before she had the chance to finish Langston had already parked and gotten out of the truck. "Are you serious?" she scoffed, put off by his actions and shift in demeanor.

Langston popped the trunk grabbing a roll of duct tape inside. Meanwhile, Cherice didn't waste any time sending out another quick text before sliding the phone into her jacket pocket.

Langston opened her car door. "Step out of the vehicle Mrs. Merriweather," he demanded.

Cherice folded her arms. "I will do no such thing."

"Yes, you will," he replied then paused for a moment. Cherice didn't budge.

"Fine…. I'll remove you myself."

"Don't you dare put your hands on me," she demanded while looking up at him with a foreboding stare.

Even so, the look in his eyes warned her not to be defiant. Cherice smacked her lips then begrudgingly stepped out of his vehicle.

Langston and Cherice walked side by side into the dimly lit, gutted, open space. "I just want you to hear me out. I know that once we are done here you will understand how fond I am of your daughter."

"I can't even think straight. You brought me to this desolate place expecting me to have compassion for you?! You were supposed to be taking me to brunch."

"Don't worry... I won't let you starve. Tell you what.... I'll go get you something to eat then we can talk. Deal?"

"And what do you expect me to do while you leave me here? Stand in the rubble?"

"No, you're going to stand right here." Langston dragged her by the arm, penning her to a steel beam that ran from the floor to the ceiling. He used duct tape rounding her body against the pole until she was affixed to it from head to ankles. Finally, he taped her mouth to stifle any pleas for rescue.

"I'll be right back." Langston bid her farewell before heading back to his vehicle.

They'd passed a cluster of restaurants on the way to the abandoned site. Figuring it couldn't have been more than five miles away it would be the safest, moreover the fastest option to go with. Langston was mindful not to speed or disobey any traffic laws, staying under the radar as much as possible. He pulled into a sandwich shop, using the drive-thru to order her food. By the time he'd made it to the pickup window it was time for a change in shift. "Damnit," he muttered through clinched teeth. "Can we hurry this up please?" he asked the cashier with angst in his tone.

The young lady smacked her lips. "We're going as fast as we can," she rebuffed, then slid the window closed.

He waited nearly fifteen minutes before being handed his order, which he snatched from her hands before pulling off. On the way back, Langston drove a little faster than he had on the way there. His anxiety was at its peak, manifesting a prickly, nagging feeling at the back of his neck. Sweat dripped from his forehead, down his brow, soaking into the collar of his shirt. The pits of his T-shirt were stained with perspiration. Langston looked left then right, behind him through the rearview mirror, then further ahead searching for those red, white and blue lights. He feared the authorities would be coming for him at any moment. Out of nowhere another vehicle blowing through the intersection ignored their red light almost plowing into Langston's vehicle. Fortunately, he was able to swerve to avoid the near collision. "Stupid mother fucker," he shouted all the while, laying in on his horn. Then out of nowhere, he stopped. His brows wrinkled. "Mr. Uncle?" Were his eyes playing tricks on him?

"I gotta chill," Langston coached himself. A couple of minutes later he arrived back at the abandoned building. He grabbed the bag then rushed inside. "Sorry it took so long," he spoke loud enough for her to hear him as he approached. But to no avail.... His statement had fallen on deaf ears.

Cherice had been freed from the duct tape and lay spayed on the concrete, dead as a door nail.

The bag dropped from his clutches upon seeing her lifeless body. "Oh my God!" Had his bottom jaw not been attached it would have hit the floor. There was only one thing he could think to say at that point.... "MR. UNCLE..."

Langston snapped back to reality just as two other gentlemen rushed in to assist. "Let's get her up off of this cold floor," one of the autopsy attendants suggested. As they lifted an unconscious Layla from the ground, Langston snatched up her cellphone. He'd need it to get Mr. Uncle aka Bruce's contact information and fast, before she'd have the opportunity to call her father notifying him of the devastating news of Cherice's murder. Langston hadn't anticipated them finding Cherice's body where he'd transported it.

While autopsy attendants carried Layla to a more comfortable room, Langston took that time to make his calls, one to Bruce and the other to Tim. Langston only hoped that he could disguise his voice enough to go undetected.

Although Langston had gotten Bruce's number from Layla's contact list, he decided against using her phone to make the calls. The phone in the sitting room at the morgue would have to do... Before punching in the first number, he pressed *67 to block out the number he was calling from.

Bruce answered without haste, "Hello."

Whatever the caller on the other end was saying caused him to take pause. Heart pounding, he sat down on the couch. Bruce's stomach turned in fear of his secret being revealed. He was terrified of going to jail, his reputation ruined...

"I'll be there," he responded, before the call was disconnected.

That's when he'd begun to recall the murder of his longtime love, Cherice.

She could hear him the moment he entered the building screaming her name. "Cherice! Baby, where are you!" he shouted.

Cherice licked at the duct tape until she could detach enough tape from her lips to scream. "Bruce, I'm here!" she shouted. "Right here." Her second outcry for rescue was much quieter than her initial plea.

It was only a moment before he came rushing toward her. "Baby, who did this to you? Did they hurt you?" He reached to take down the duct tape from her mouth completely. "You got some of it off, baby."

"I licked it," she responded mouth now fully exposed.

"Who did this?" Bruce proceeded to unravel the tape binding the length of her body.

"Just get me out of here before he comes back. I'll explain everything later," she demanded.

"I can't believe I could have lost you. I'm never letting you go, again. I'm so glad you chose me." He babbled on while freeing her.

"What are you going on about? I'm going to have to go home."

"Home?" Bruce looked confused.

"I thought this meant we would finally be together. Then why didn't you call Tim?"

Her brows wrinkled. Cherice was irritated and ready to leave.

"Because I was supposed to be meeting up with you today."

"Why was I never good enough for you? I'm smarter, better looking and I know you get along better with me. I even make more money than him. Would it be so terrible being with me?" He ranted while pacing back and forth.

"I want to leave this place. Please, take me away from here." Cherice attempted to walk by, but Bruce grabbed her arms with both hands then forced her back toward the metal beam she'd been taped to.

"Are you crazy?" At first, she stared at him in shock, yet the expression fleeted giving way to anger. Her face contorted. "Don't you ever put your paws on me!"

"Oh, now I'm a dog? First, you basically say I'm not fit to be your husband. Now you're calling me a dog?" He fumed.

With her chin held high she responded, "Only an animal would put his hands on a woman. Why would I be with you?" she spat.

He wanted to cry, and she could see it. Cherice smirked cluing him into that fact. His feelings were hurt, moreover ego bruised. It only took a second before his large hands were wrapped around her neck, strangling the life out of her. The veins in the side of her head protruded. Her face burned red. Cherice's eyes rolled back up into their lids before her neck muscles released allowing her head to slump to the side. She was dead and he knew it. Bruce loosened his grip, and her corpse dropped to the floor.

"Why did you make me do this, Cherice?! Why?!" he shouted, on the brink of hysteria. "Oh my God... I can't be here; I can't be here." Bruce shook his head in disbelief before bolting from the scene of the crime. He had murdered his one true love...

That was the realization he recalled before his consciousness emerged. He was back from the horrible trip down memory lane with an even bigger problem on his hands. The time had come to go back to see what he'd left behind, more importantly who had witnessed his crime.

Over at the Merriweather residence Tim mopped his kitchen floor free of the corn syrup used to simulate fake blood in the misdelivered package. Detective Vernon stood in the driveway finishing up his questioning of the neighbor. He'd figured since he had him there he may as well ask about the last time he'd seen Cherice.

A loud buzz from the house phone simultaneously startled Tim and alerted the detective.

Tim rushed over to answer the call. "Hello."

Detective Vernon entered through the side door, hoping whoever was on the other end could shed light on Mrs. Merriweather's whereabouts. There wasn't much he could decipher from Tim's responses to the caller.

"Yes, I understand…… okay… I'll be there," Tim assured the mystery caller before the call disconnected.

Detective Vernon stepped closer. "Any news regarding your wife?"

"Uh… no, that was just my doctor confirming my next appointment."

Detective Vernon wanted to believe him but the look in his eyes, moreover the hesitation in his tone said otherwise. Even so, the detective decided against further questioning. He had ways of getting around the deception of others.

"I'm sorry, Tim. I'm gonna head back to the office to see if there are any new developments."

"Please, let me know immediately if you find out anything."

"I won't hesitate," Detective Vernon replied.

Before springing into action, Tim waited for him to leave, then watched out of the window as he drove up the block. Little did he know Detective Vernon merely rounded the corner. He planned on waiting to see if Tim was going to leave the house so he could further surveil Mr. Merriweather.

Twenty minutes later, Tim emerged from his house with a satchel tight across his chest. He looked determined yet uncomfortable, adjusting it a few times before he'd finally made it to his vehicle.

Detective Vernon waited for him to get going and around the corner before taking pursuit. He remained a good distance behind to prevent his cover from being blown, but Tim was vigilant, checking every mirror before and after each unnecessary turn he'd made. By the third turn Detective Vernon had been made. Tim sped up, creating a considerable distance between them along with several vehicles. It had become increasingly difficult for the detective to keep up. He lost him over the railroad track, an Amtrack holding him up amongst a line of other vehicles.

For a moment, Tim relaxed having accomplished what he deemed a great feat, then within seconds dread over the possibility of finding his wife hurt washed over him. He tried to remain optimistic, but he knew the situation could end in tragedy. As Tim approached the location, he'd been instructed to go to his eyes grew wide with shock before his face twisted into an angry scowl. "She's been with him all along," he fumed. Tim tore through the semi graveled parking lot. Dust and gravel shot through the air as he came to a halt at the abandoned building's entrance and next to Bruce's vehicle.

Tim snatched the hollowed out door of the dilapidated building open, tearing into the dimly lit open space. "Show your face, muthafucka," he demanded.

"Here I am," Bruce uttered from behind him as he wielded the two by four down on the back of Tim's head.

Tim crashed to the cement floor. He lay there seemingly unconscious. "Get up, tough guys. You may have been able to bully Cherice into staying with you, but you can't bully me. This is all your fault. Now neither one of us will have her."

His admission shattered Tim's heart. He knew that meant his Cherice was gone. Tim needed time to come back from the daze he was in due to the blow to his head before making a snap decision that could cost him his life as well. Bruce snatched up one of Tim's legs then began dragging him toward the center of the space where Cherice once lay.

"Why did you do it? Why did you kill my wife?"

Bruce dropped Tim's leg. "Your wife…" he paused "Your wife has been my lover longer than she's been your wife."

"If that's the truth then that makes you look even more like a desperate loser. Second string… just couldn't make the cut, huh…. I guess she was telling the truth about something. In her eyes you just weren't husband material."

Bruce was livid. He grabbed the nine-millimeter he'd tucked into the waist belt of his pants. Unfortunately for him, it wasn't faster than Tim whipped out his .38 snub nose revolver from under the satchel he pulled it from while being dragged across the floor. One, Two, Three, Four, Five, shots rang out. The bullets pierced through Bruce's torso as he stumbled back into the darkness.

Over at the morgue, Langston was busy comforting a now conscious Layla. She cried, seeking comfort in his arms. "I'm here, Layla baby. I'm so sorry this happened." He caressed and held her close. "I promise, I'm here for you. I'll never leave."

If it was the last thing Langston did, he'd prove to Layla that he was indeed, husband material.

Cherice's POV – By: Octavia Grant

Octavia Grant discovered her love of creative writing at the age of sixteen. She began writing professionally in 2016, two years later she decided to take the reins of her literary career and became an Independent Author. As an Independent Author, Octavia has penned over 30 novels. She's been interviewed by Narrator iiKane, interviewed by Literary Reviewer and Movie Commentator Tamara Walker of Tam Telling Tales, featured in magazines WYB Lifestyle, Voyage Jacksonville, Canvas Rebel, named in 160 Black Women In Horror as well as the winner of the It's Lit Award for Best Black Mystery/Suspense.

Good morning, Beautiful. Just checking in. Making sure we're still on for the day.

Cherice blushed as she read her text message. The number was not saved in her phone. It didn't need to be. She had memorized the ten digits years ago. Butterflies fluttered in her stomach at the thought of how good her day would be. She felt silly as she danced around like a girl with a crush. But this person, this person just did something to her nervous system. Electricity traveled through every inch of her body at the mere thought of things to come. With her cheeks aching from smiling, Cherice began to text quickly. Her fingers flying over the keyboard as if it had wings.

Yes Honey. We're still on for the day. Tim thinks I'll be at the Spa. TTYL.

Cherice chuckled at her use of the acronym for Talk To You Later. She knew Layla would be in disbelief if she ever found out how tech savvy and hip and cool she truly was.

"Do people still say hip and cool?" Cherice asked herself as she erased the text thread.

She laughed again as she thought of her choice of words. She hadn't kept up with the newest lingo, but she knew for sure that she had never once heard her daughter use the phrase hip and cool. Cherice couldn't care less about the term being amongst today's list of popular words.

Her mind just thought of random things anytime she saw the number. Thinking of random things was just a way to calm her nerves. She wasn't nervous. It was the excitement, the thought of things to come, that threatened to push her over the edge.

Going into her closet, Cherice pulled out her olive green Fabletics Yoga outfit. She had never done Yoga; it was just something comfortable she wore to run errands. After grabbing her outfit, she peeked outside the closet to make sure that Tim was nowhere in sight. Realizing that the coast was clear, she pulled her shoe rack from the wall and opened the tied Walmart bag. Panties, not the Hanes or Fruit Of The Loom, that she wore around her husband. No, today required something special.

Goosebumps covered her flesh as her fingers caressed the lacy fabric of the Joyspun Brand cheeky panties and matching bra. She knew she wouldn't be wearing them long. But there was something so sexy about being seen and complimented. If she ever wore something like this for Tim, he'd start an argument or start hurling accusations.

His insecurities, lack of drive to do anything fun or thrilling had always turned her off. She couldn't deny that even though he had his quirks, she loved him, but he just wasn't enough. He had settled into the comfortable stage years ago and had no desire to ever leave. She was ashamed to admit that with her husband, she was simply existing, not living.

"Oh well." Cherice shrugged as she made her way to the bathroom to shower. Her days of feeling guilty were over a long time ago. Today was her day to get pampered and she refused to dampen her good mood with thoughts of her cranky husband.

Grabbing her Fragrance-Free Dove body wash, she bathed every inch of her body. She didn't want to use her normal shea butter body wash because she didn't want to mix fragrances. The only scent she wanted to smell was the vanilla and jasmine oil that would soon be drizzled on her skin.

There was no need to take the long shower that she'd normally take. That would take too much time. All she needed today was ten minutes. Lotion was another thing she refused to use. That took too much time, and she was ready to get to her destination.

Stepping out of the shower, she grabbed her towel and dried off quickly. Popping the tags off her department store lingerie, she flushed it down the toilet instead of putting it in the trash. There had been times when she caught Tim going through the trash looking for who knows what.

Looking in the mirror she smiled at her reflection. She couldn't deny that she liked what she saw. The lace looked amazing against her skin.

"Not too shabby," Cherice thought as she winked at her reflection.

She stepped into her yoga outfit in mere seconds and opened the bathroom door. She wasn't surprised when she saw Tim sitting on the bed. Inwardly, she rolled her eyes. Outwardly, she wore her normal sweet and friendly smile.

"Hey Honey. Coming to see me off?" Cherice asked as she walked up to him and planted a kiss on his forehead.

"You look nice in that green. I know you wear this all the time, but it really looks nice on you,"

The compliment stunned her. Giving compliments wasn't something that Tim did often or ever. He was the type of person that assumed a person should know how they looked.

"Thank you, Tim," she said sincerely. She couldn't believe that the compliment truly did warm her heart. But not enough to make her change her plans. "I've already cooked dinner and fixed your plate. All you have to do is remove the foil from the plate and turn the microwave on," Cherice said as she placed a kiss directly onto his lips. Yes, she had plans. But she still had to take care of home first.

"I don't know what I'd do without you CeCe," Tim said truthfully. "You know, I don't understand that spa stuff and massages. But it's important to you, so it's important to me. Here you go," Tim said as he handed Cherice three crisp one-hundred-dollar bills.

Cherice's head was spinning. Where did this new version of her husband come from? She was confused and unsure of how to proceed. Anger instantly filled her. Though she knew she shouldn't have, she asked a question and instantly regretted it.

"Are you having an affair?"

Tim threw his head back and laughed.

"I'm too old and too lazy to have an affair. Enjoy your massage, honey."

Embarrassment filled Cherice. She couldn't even look in his face. With what she had planned, she knew she had no right to ask such a disrespectful question, but she couldn't stop the words from coming out of her mouth. Tim's behavior just caught her off guard. Giving away cash was unlike her husband. Yes, he paid all the bills, but somehow, he believed her self-care was her responsibility.

"I guess you can teach an old dog new tricks," Cherice thought as she placed the money in her cars cup holder.

"Hey Siri, text 312-555-4517"

"What would you like to say?"

"Be there in thirty minutes."

A reply message came back instantly.

"Hey Siri, read the text from 312-555-4517."

"I'm already here. Your key is at the front desk."

Cherice placed her foot on the gas. Cutting the thirty-minute drive down to nineteen minutes. She could barely sit still as she drove to her destination. As soon as she saw the Hilton at Airport Blvd, sweat began to form under her arms as her body temperature increased. Besides the spa, this hotel had become her favorite place. Though travelers kept the area busy, she felt secure here and never had to worry about being exposed, because Tim wasn't into flights and traveling.

Turning off her phone's location, she placed her phone in her purse and walked to the front desk.

"Greetings, Mrs. Merriweather," the front desk clerk said before Cherice could even state her name. He slid the room key to her without asking for an ID, because he, like many of the other front desk clerks knew exactly who she was. Cherice offered a polite smile and nod, then speed walked to the elevator bay. Excitement made her dance on the tips of her toes. When the silver doors slid open, she practically ran inside the elevator.

She pounded on the number 4 hoping that the harder she hit the button the faster she'd be taken to her destination. Cherice hated to admit it, but she felt like a fiend. This feeling was so addictive that she couldn't contain herself, nor did she want to.

DING!

As soon as the door opened, Cherice ran down the hotel corridor as if her name were Flo Jo. Wasting no time, she swiped her key and unlocked the door.

The scent of fresh fruit and vanilla scented candles invaded her nostrils. Her nipples hardened to the point where it felt as if it would cut through the fabric of her Fabletics jacket. She removed it and threw it on the high back chair.

"You really know how to set the mood. I've been waiting all day to see you."

"*So, have I.*"

At the sound of the masculine voice that came from behind her back, Cherice turned and screamed. She quickly reached for her jacket to cover her laced covered breast, but he was quicker.

"Wha..what are you doing here? It's not... it's not what you think,"

He didn't say a word. He simply admired the beauty of the woman he once loved and now hated.

"How could you do this to me?" He asked, his voice trembling, tears filling his eyes.

Cherice trembled.

For as long as she had known this man, the one thing she knew was tears was not a good sign.

"I can explain."

"Explain? I'd love to hear the explanation of why you were in a hotel to meet my wife!" Bruce screamed as he threw the jacket into Cherice's face.

She screamed.

"Bruce, I'm sorry-"

"Imagine my surprise, when I found out that the woman that I had an affair with was sleeping with my wife,"

Cherice looked away in shame. She couldn't deny it. For the past two years, she and Ramona Canton had been meeting at this hotel twice a month. At her age, she never thought she'd entertain something so taboo, but she had.

After finding out about the affair, Ramona had confronted her in the hotel parking garage, then burst into tears. Cherice felt horrible. Bruce was her high school sweetheart. Moments with him were simply a walk down memory lane.

Yes, she knew he was married, but she never inquired about his wife because his wife was his responsibility, not hers. She didn't want to steal him away from her; she only wanted moments just to reminisce. But at the sight of Ramona's beautiful face covered in the hurt that she caused, Cherice only wanted to make her feel better.

Wiping her tears, Cherice invaded Ramona's space and began to plant kisses where her tears had been. Ramona was shocked, but surprisingly, she allowed everything to happen.

"Bruce, this-,"

Ring! Ring!

The sound of Cherice's blaring phone interrupted her speech. Though she didn't want to speak with him, she answered the phone anyway.

"Hey, Langston"

"Mrs. Merriweather, I'm sorry to bother you. I just wanted to clear the air. There's been a big misunderstanding between me and Layla. Some girl kissed me and-"

"Langston, I'm a little busy. Just explain to Lay what happened and give her a couple of days to cool off. I really have to go Langston," Cherice said before ending the call. She wasn't in the mood to help him fix anything. Not when she had her own issue to fix.

"Bruce, I'm-"

"I don't want to hear any lies that come from your mouth. When you ended our affair, I respected your decision. I understood that you had a family, just like I did, and you didn't want to lose them. Like I didn't want to lose mine. So, imagine my shock and horror when I discovered text messages, pictures, and videos of my wife doing things to my mistress and vice versa!" Bruce screamed as he kicked the table.

"Bruce, I'm sorry. It won't happen again. It was a mistake." Cherice couldn't understand why referring to the acts that she and Ramona shared as a mistake felt so wrong. She wouldn't call their situation love, but she had a special place in her heart for Ramona, and truthfully, she didn't want to give her up. Yes, they were lovers, but they were also genuine friends.

"Oh, I know it won't," Bruce said as he showed Cherice the photo of his wife.

Cherice screamed as she looked at the picture of Ramona. Her chest appeared to have exploded. In the picture, Bruce smiled as his dead wife stared lifelessly at nothing.

"She ripped my heart out, so I had to return the favor. If I'm going to be in pain, Timothy is going to be in pain too," Bruce said maniacally as he plunged the already blood covered knife into Cherice's chest.

Bad Intentions - By: Toni LaRue'

Meet Toni Larue', the creative force behind captivating suspense

 novels that have kept countless readers at the edge of their seats. The Bay Area native introduces a refreshing and rejuvenating element to the thriller genre by deftly crafting compelling narratives and evocative African American characters that linger long after you put the book down.

Toni Larue' was born and raised in Richmond, California and later relocated to Las Vegas, Nevada where she now lives with her husband.

Present - Day 6 (Morning) - Layla

Layla's eyes fluttered open to a world that seemed too bright. Harsh fluorescent lights buzzed overhead, casting strange shadows across unfamiliar walls. Her thoughts came in fragments, pieces of consciousness slowly knitting themselves together: the antiseptic smell, the steady beep of monitors. Hospital. She was in the hospital.

Through the fog of confusion, she became aware of Langston's presence beside her. He sat perfectly still except for his fingers which tapped an uneven rhythm on the armrest - tap-tap-pause-tap - like morse code spelling out some hidden message. His eyes never left her face, watching with an intensity that seemed oddly out of place.

"Where..." The word felt thick in her throat, her mouth desert dry.

"You collapsed in the morgue," Langston's voice came soft. "The doctors say it was probably stress and exhaustion. With everything that's happening with your mom."

Mom.

The word crashed through her consciousness, shattering the fog. Memory flooded back with brutal clarity: Six days. Six days since her mother had vanished without a trace. Six days of jumping at every phone call. Six days of her father's face growing more haunted with each passing hour. Six days of not knowing whether to grieve or hope.

"It wasn't her," Langston said, leaning forward taking her hand.

Relief washed over her, followed immediately by guilt - even if it wasn't her mother, someone's loved one lay in that morgue. But the questions remained, burning in her mind: Where was her mother? Why hadn't she called?

"Have the police found anything?"

"Nothing yet," he murmured. "They're still looking."

"I just want this to be over," she said, trying to pull her hand away, but his grip remained firm.

"I know, babe." He kissed her hand, his lips lingering. "I hate seeing you like this. But you know I'll always be here for you. Always."

Before Layla could respond, her phone buzzed on the bedside table, the sound startling in the quiet room. As she reached for it, Langston's hand shot out with unexpected speed. "You should rest," he said, voice tight. "I'll check it for you."

"It might be my dad."

"And I'll tell him you're resting." He smiled as he picked up her phone, positioning it so she couldn't see the screen. "You need to focus on getting better. Let me take care of everything else."

Before - Cherice

Five Days Earlier...

Cherice Merriweather stood at her kitchen window, watching dawn paint the sky in watercolor strokes of pink and gold. Steam no longer rose from her forgotten coffee – she'd been standing there for hours, replaying yesterday's scene in her mind. Like a video clip stuck on loop: Langston, the strange woman, the way something felt profoundly wrong.

"You're up early again." Tim's voice startled her. She hadn't heard him come downstairs.

"Couldn't sleep," she murmured, fingers tightening around her cup. "Tim, we need to talk about Langston."

Her husband moved beside her, his aftershave familiar and comforting. "The boyfriend? What about him?"

"I saw him yesterday while running errands." Cherice turned, meeting Tim's eyes. "With another woman."

Tim's expression sharpened. "Are you sure?"

"I'm positive." Her voice was steady. "They looked... intimate. The way he touched her arm, how close they stood. Close enough to kiss." She reached for her phone. "I took pictures."

"Have you told Layla?"

"No. I wanted to talk to her in person." She swallowed. "But that's not all. You know how I've been saying something about him isn't right? I decided to look into him a little bit."

"You did what?" Tim's frown deepened. "Cherice—"

"And it's more than the woman, Tim." The words tumbled out now, urgent. "Haven't you noticed how he appeared in Layla's life? No warning, no introduction through friends. Just suddenly there, knowing her schedule, showing up everywhere she goes. Lay thinks it's cute. But sometimes..." She hesitated, remembering moments that had made her skin crawl. "Sometimes I catch him watching her when he thinks no one's looking. Not like a boyfriend watching his girlfriend. Like..."

"Like what?"

She shook her head, unable to put the creeping dread into words.

"Look, babe. Let me look into it," Tim said finally, his tone gentler. "Through official channels. But you need to step back."

"Tim—"

"I mean it, Cherice. If there's something to find, I'll find it. But running your own investigation could make things worse."

She wanted to argue to make him understand the darkness she sensed lurking behind Langston's perfect facade. But she recognized that set to his jaw – he'd made up his mind.

"Fine," she said. "You look into it. But promise me you won't brush this off."

"I won't." He kissed her forehead, lingering a moment. "I have to head to the office. Try not to worry so much."

As Tim's footsteps faded, Cherice turned back to the window. A black sedan she didn't recognize sat across the street.

Present – Day 6 (Afternoon) - Langston

Langston watched Layla's chest rise and fall with each breath, his fingers unconsciously curling at his side, remembering. The moon cast shadows across her sleeping form, painting her in shades of silver and blue. So peaceful now. So trusting. Her mother had been right about one thing – he did watch Layla. Had been watching her for months, learning every habit, every preference, every vulnerability.

He reached out, brushing a strand of hair from her face with gentle fingers, hoping not to wake her. Her skin was warm beneath his fingertips, alive with possibility. So different from Cherice's final moments – the wild terror in her eyes, the desperate scratches at his hands, the way understanding had dawned too late. She'd thought she was protecting her daughter. She never understood that Layla was already his.

Beatrice's interference had been unexpected – those desperate hang-up calls to Layla and her parent's house, that kiss. All attempts to drive him and Layla apart. He hadn't lied when he told Layla about the kiss; Beatrice had kissed him, trying to rekindle what they'd had. But she'd become a liability, feeding Cherice's suspicions, threatening everything he'd built.

Layla stirred, a soft "Mom?" escaping her lips. Langston's hand froze mid-caress, muscles coiling tight. But she only shifted, settling deeper into dreams. Soon she'd stop asking about Cherice.

He traced the curve of her cheek, remembering how Cherice had looked at him that day – suspicion hardening into certainty. She'd thought she was so clever, listening to Beatrice, gathering her little bits of proof. She never understood that when it came to Layla, there was nothing he wouldn't do. No line he wouldn't cross.

Before - Cherice

The woman in the dark sedan hadn't moved for fifteen minutes, but Cherice didn't need her to. She knew exactly who it was—the same stranger she'd seen with Langston just days ago while running errands. The large, unmistakable head of curls gave her away.

Before Cherice could stop herself she was already crossing the street. The immaculate lawn of her Tudor-style home felt miles away now, receding behind her as adrenaline pushed her forward.

She rapped her knuckles against the driver's window, her heart hammering in her chest. Forcing confidence into her voice, she asked, "Can I help you?"

The window slid down with a soft, electronic whir, revealing a woman in her early twenties. A gold nameplate necklace glinted against her collarbone. Beatrice.

"You're Layla's mother." It wasn't a question. Her eyes darted nervously to the rearview mirror before returning to Cherice. "Please—we need to talk, but not here. Not out in the open."

Cherice's brow furrowed. "Who are you?"

The woman hesitated, as if calculating how much to say. "Beatrice." She killed the engine and climbed out of the car, her movements clumsy and uncertain. "I know this seems… strange, but it's about Langston. It's important."

Cherice studied her carefully, suspicion knotting her brows tighter. But something in Beatrice's tone—urgent, almost desperate—pulled her in.

Without a word, Cherice gestured toward the front garden, where mature hydrangeas created a natural privacy screen. They moved toward the shelter of the bushes, the early morning air carrying a bite that made Cherice pull her cardigan tighter around herself.

"Start talking," Cherice said, her tone sharp.

"I've been trying to work up the courage," Beatrice admitted, her perfectly manicured hands twisting together. "Those calls to your house—hanging up when anyone answered? That was me. I just... I couldn't find the words."

"You wanted to talk to me about Langston?" Cherice asked, cutting straight to the point.

Beatrice's grip on Cherice's arm was sudden and surprisingly strong. "Listen carefully." Her voice dropped to a near-whisper. "Get your daughter away from him. The charming student, the perfect boyfriend—it's all fake. Every move, every word. I know because I fell for it, too."

"You and he…"

"Were together, yes. Until I saw behind the mask." Beatrice's voice trembled. "There's something wrong with him. The way he becomes obsessed, how he isolates you so subtly you don't even notice until you're completely alone. And when you try to leave…" Her voice broke as she pulled back her shirt sleeve, revealing a pale scar that circled her wrist like a bracelet of bad memories.

Cherice's stomach churned. "Why come to me? Why not warn Layla directly?"

Beatrice's laugh was bitter and humorless. "He's already poisoned that well. I'm just the crazy ex-girlfriend who can't let go—that's how he's painted me to her. Anything I say will only push her closer to him."

"I saw you…" Cherice started. "The two of you looked—close."

"He showed up where I was." The admission came quickly. "I was being pleasant to keep him from getting angry. You don't want to see Langston angry."

Beatrice's eyes darted to the end of the street, her body tensing at the sight of a neighbor walking their dog. Her paranoia was palpable. "I shouldn't stay. He has ways of knowing things, of showing up exactly when you don't expect him."

She pulled out her phone and, moments later, Cherice's phone buzzed in her pocket. "Save my number in case you have questions."

Beatrice took a step back, retreating toward her car.

"Wait," Cherice called as Beatrice opened the driver's door. "How do I know you're telling the truth?"

Beatrice paused, her hand gripping the doorframe. The fear in her eyes deepened into something darker, something closer to terror. "Because I'm still looking over my shoulder all these months later. Get Layla away from him. Before it's too late."

The Mercedes purred to life and peeled away leaving Cherice standing in the street alone. Her hands were shaking as she pulled out her phone and dialed Layla's number. Each ring stretched like an eternity until her daughter's voice finally filled the line.

"Hey, Mom."

"Hi, baby. I just wanted to—" Cherice steadied her voice, trying to sound casual. "After my appointment at Lovely Touch this afternoon, I need to talk to you about something important. About Langston."

She could almost hear her daughter rolling her eyes. "Mom, I can't. I have to study, and I really don't want to talk about him right now."

"Layla, please—"

"We can talk tomorrow, okay? Love you!"

The line went dead before Cherice could respond. She stared at her phone, her daughter's dismissive tone ringing in her ears.

As she headed toward the house to get dressed and hopefully be taken as a walk-in at the spa, her phone buzzed again.

"Hello?" she answered.

"It's Langston," said the voice on the other end. "I need to talk to you about Layla."

Present - Day 6 - Layla

Layla feigned sleep while her mind raced. She kept her breathing steady, fighting the urge to open her eyes. Langston was there - she could feel his presence, hear the slight shift of his weight in the chair beside her bed.

Her mother's last words echoed in her mind. After my appointment at Lovely Touch, I need to talk to you about something important...about Langston. The memory of brushing her off with a quick "love you" twisted like a knife in her gut. If only she'd made time to talk. If only she'd noticed something was wrong in her mother's voice.

The steady beep of hospital monitors filled the silence. Down the hall, nurses' shoes squeaked against linoleum. She focused on these sounds trying to ground herself in the present, but her thoughts kept drifting.

Had her mother discovered something about Langston? She knew he was the last to talk to her, but was he the last to see her?

Before - Cherice

Instead of trying to get a walk-in appointment at Lovely Touch, Cherice found herself sitting in her car, parked in a vacant lot near the airport waiting for Langston. He had insisted on meeting her here, claiming he needed to be on this side of town anyway, so she agreed to meet him.

Apparently, Layla had caught him and Beatrice together at a bookstore. He swore it was innocent—claimed Beatrice kissed him and it meant nothing—but Cherice wasn't stupid. She knew the truth, or at least enough to know he was lying.

As Langston climbed into the passenger seat, Cherice sighed and pulled out her phone to text Tim about her whereabouts. Her stomach dropped when she realized there was no cell service out there. Great, she thought as she placed her phone back into her purse.

"I swear, I would never do anything to hurt Layla. You have to make her see that," Langston said, his voice already carrying a desperate edge. He fidgeted with the zipper on his jacket, avoiding her gaze.

Cherice stared at him for a moment, weighing her words. "Now that I'm looking at things, Langston… maybe it's best the two of you spent some time apart. Focus on school. You're young. Layla doesn't need this kind of stress in her life."

Langston's head snapped toward her. "I love Layla, Cherice." His voice cracked slightly, but his words were firm.

Cherice narrowed her eyes, refusing to let his sudden vulnerability sway her. "Love doesn't look like this, Langston. Love isn't sneaking around with another woman and then lying about it."

"I'm not sneaking around!" he shouted, the vein on his forehead pulsing as his frustration boiled over. "Beatrice kissed me, okay? I didn't ask for it, I didn't want it, and I pushed her away. But Layla didn't even give me a chance to explain!"

Cherice folded her arms across her chest. "And why exactly were you even with Beatrice in the first place? If you're so innocent, why didn't you tell Layla about it before she caught you? You think I don't know how this works?"

Langston groaned, running his hands over his face. "I wasn't with her, Cherice! She showed up at the bookstore, started talking to me, and I was trying to be polite!"

"Polite?" Cherice scoffed, her tone dripping with sarcasm. "Polite is holding the door open for someone. Polite is saying 'excuse me.' Polite is not letting your ex get close enough to kiss you!"

Langston clenched his jaw, his nostrils flaring. "I didn't let her do anything! Why are you acting like I planned this? Like I don't care about Layla? You know me better than that."

"Do I?" Cherice shot back, her voice rising. "Because from where I'm sitting, you care more about your ego than you do about Layla's feelings. You knew exactly how this would look, Langston, and you didn't care enough to stop it."

Langston slammed his fist against the dashboard, making Cherice flinch. "That's not true!" he yelled. "I care about her more than anything—more than anyone! And I'm not going to let you or anyone else tell me I don't!"

Cherice took a deep breath to calm herself, refusing to let his outburst intimidate her. "If you really cared about her, you'd stop being so selfish. Layla deserves someone who makes her feel safe, someone who puts her first. Right now, you're not that person, Langston."

His eyes burned into hers, his hands trembling in his lap. "I am that person. I love her, Cherice. I'll do whatever it takes to prove that to her. But don't you dare think for one second that anyone—anyone—is going to keep me away from Layla. Not you, not Beatrice, not anyone."

The finality in his tone sent a chill down Cherice's spine. She opened her mouth to respond, but the words wouldn't come. Langston's gaze was unwavering, his determination almost unsettling.

Present - Day 6 - Layla

Through heavy eyelids, Layla watched a nurse check her vitals.

"I gave you something to help you sleep," the nurse said. "But let me know if you feel any discomfort, okay?"

Layla nodded—her throat too dry for words. The nurse double-checked the monitor and patted her hand before heading toward the door.

"I'll be back in about an hour to check on you again," the nurse added before slipping out, the door clicking shut behind her.

The quiet settled again, broken only by the faint tapping of Langston's fingers against her phone screen. He sat in the chair by the window, hunched over her phone, scrolling as if it might reveal something important.

Layla's lips parted—her voice hoarse from disuse. "Any messages from Dad?"

Langston's head shot up, guilt flashing across his face for a split second before he composed himself. He turned the phone screen toward her, showing an empty notification bar. "No. Nothing yet."

Layla frowned, her brow furrowing. "Give me my phone," she said, her voice rasping but firm. She attempted to lift herself up despite the heaviness in her limbs. "I want to call him myself."

Langston leaned forward, his hands gripping the edge of the bed rail. "Layla, listen to me. He's not going to do anything except freak out and make this worse. I'm handling it, okay? I'm here. That's all that matters."

Layla blinked at him, too tired to summon the anger bubbling beneath the surface. But his words gnawed at her, and her voice came stronger than she expected. "I'd like to call him myself."

"Layla—"

"Now."

Langston stood, towering over her bed with a posture that made her stomach twist. "Layla," he said again, softer this time, but with an edge that felt more like a warning.

She reached for the call button by her bedside, but his hand darted out faster, his fingers wrapping around her wrist. Not hurting but restraining. This wasn't her gentle, protective boyfriend. This was someone else entirely.

"Let go," she said, her voice trembling. The heart monitor betrayed her fear, its beeping accelerating to match her racing pulse.

"We should talk about this when you're calmer," Langston said, his grip remaining firm. "When you're thinking more rationally."

"I want you to leave," she said, her words shaking but determined. "Now."

The look Langston gave her made her blood run cold. Because in that split second before he composed himself, she saw it: rage. Pure, unmasked rage.

"I think we need some space," Layla said, her voice barely above a whisper.

Langston moved toward the door, but instead of leaving, he closed it with a soft, deliberate click.

"Space to think about what, exactly?" His voice was low, cold, and unfamiliar.

"About everything," Layla said, her throat tightening. "Mom's disappearance, the way you've been acting—" She fought to keep her voice steady despite her racing heart. "I just... I just need time."

Langston crossed the room in two smooth steps, his presence looming over her. "There's nothing to think about," he said as his hand came to rest on her shoulder, too heavy to feel comforting. "Your mother abandoned you. You know that. I'm all you have now."

Layla froze as his fingers slid from her shoulder to her throat, not squeezing but resting there with a weight that felt like a warning.

"Careful, Layla." His thumb stroked the pulse point on her neck, feeling the frantic rhythm beneath his touch. "You're still quite fragile. Anything could happen." His eyes bore into hers, unblinking and devoid of the warmth she once knew. "We wouldn't want that, would we?"

His fingers flexed against her throat, just enough to make her breath hitch. In that moment, with a terrifying clarity, Layla knew exactly what had happened to her mother.

Before - Cherice

The car fell silent, the air between them thick with unspoken threats. The distant hum of planes overhead was the only sound, but even that felt muted in the weight of the moment.

Cherice's chest rose and fell as she tried to steady her breathing. She glanced down at her purse, where her phone was tucked away, useless without service. Against her better judgment, she decided to push him further.

"Langston," she said, her voice low but firm, "if you really love her, you'd let her go. You're only hurting her at this point."

His head snapped to her, his expression darkening in an instant. "You don't know what you're talking about."

"I know enough," Cherice said, meeting his gaze despite the unease creeping up her spine. "I know that whatever you're trying to prove, it's not about Layla. It's about control. And she deserves better than that."

He laughed—the sound devoid of humor. "I'm not going anywhere." He leaned back in his seat, his hands gripping his knees. "But you are."

Cherice's fingers fumbled for the door handle, her instincts screaming at her to run, but Langston was faster. His hand shot out, grabbing her wrist in a bruising grip.

"Where do you think you're going?" he asked, his voice menacing.

"Let go of me."

"You've been trying to get rid of me since the beginning," he said, his voice low and steady. "But you can't. Layla loves me. She'll always love me. And no matter what you say or do, she's mine."

Cherice clawed at his hand, panic setting in as his other hand moved to her throat. The world tilted as he squeezed, cutting off her air.

"You'll never get away with this," she choked out, her voice barely audible.

Langston's lips curled into a sneer. "I already have."

Cherice's vision blurred as blackness crept in from the edges. Her hands weakened, falling away from his wrist as her strength faded.

"Layla will never..." she gasped, clinging to the last shred of air.

"Layla will never know."

Before - Langston

He pulled on the black latex gloves with a snap against the wrists. Cherice's body was already wrapped and hidden deep in the wooded area where no one would think to look. Now for the finishing touch.

Her car gleamed under the parking lot lights at the Airport. Long-term parking – where hundreds of vehicles sat while their owners jetted off to new lives. The perfect place for someone to abandon their old one.

The weight of her phone felt heavy in his pocket as he slid into the driver's seat. He'd already drafted the texts to her friends and family. Little breadcrumbs suggesting she'd been planning this.

"You really should have been more careful with your passwords, Cherice," he murmured, readjusting the seat as if Cherice had always been behind the wheel. (Mention password was Layla's birthday)

He got out, wiped down every surface he'd touched, and placed her purse on the passenger seat. Inside, her wallet still held her ID, credit cards, everything a person would need to start over. And her phone.

"You brought this on yourself," he said to the empty car. "You should have just stayed out of it."

By morning, people would be looking for Cherice Merriweather. They'd find her car here, assume she'd fled.

And he would be there for Layla, holding her through her grief, helping her accept that sometimes people just leave. That sometimes the only one you can truly count on is the one right beside you.

Before - Beatrice

Her hands didn't shake as she wrapped the package. They should have, given what was inside, but rage had a way of steadying them. The box addressed to Tim Merriweather felt heavy under her fingers, but not as heavy as the fury coursing through her veins.

"You promised," she whispered, her voice trembling with quiet venom. Langston's face flashed in her mind—his lies, his charm, the way he'd spoken to her like she was the only one who truly mattered. "You said it was just a game. That we were forever."

But that was before Layla. Before he decided to throw away three years of them for some… some bitch who didn't understand him like she did.

She'd watched him with Cherice. He thought he was smart, but she was brilliant. She knew showing up at Layla's parents' house would push him, would make him act irrationally. And she'd been right.

She'd followed him after that argument. Watched him lose control. Watched him choke the life out of that woman and bury her deep in the woods, where he thought no one would find her. He did all of that for Layla.

And now, she'd do something for him.

"You'll see," she murmured, her voice soft as she placed the box on Cherice's front porch, its gruesome contents hidden beneath the wrapping paper. The decapitated head inside was neatly arranged, her work meticulous. "You'll remember who really understands you."

When Tim opened the package, when the police came, they'd look at Langston first.

She smiled, a small, satisfied curve of her lips. Langston had always been so good at making her feel special, at teaching her to embrace the darkness inside her. But he'd forgotten one thing—she'd learned too well.

"You'll come back," she whispered, her hand lingering on the doorbell before pressing it. She turned and walked briskly back to her car, the weight of revenge heavy in her heart but her steps light.

"When she's gone, when you're alone..." Her voice softened to a murmur as she climbed into the driver's seat, the engine purring to life. She smiled again, her fingers tightening on the wheel. "You'll remember us."

Present - Day 6 (Evening) - Layla

Black spots danced at the edges of her vision as Langston's fingers dug deeper into her throat. The frantic beeping of the heart monitor seemed distant now, fading like everything else.

"I sacrificed everything for you," he snarled, his face inches from hers. His voice was raw, almost unhinged. "All to keep you. To protect you."

The door burst open. Through dimming consciousness, Layla saw a figure she recognized—wild dark hair, blazing eyes. Beatrice.

"Get away from her!" Beatrice's voice cut through the haze like a blade. In her hand was a scalpel—likely stolen from a supply cart.

Langston's grip loosened just enough for Layla to suck in a desperate gulp of air. "You shouldn't be here," he said, his voice eerily calm despite the chaos.

"Neither should you." Beatrice's laugh was sharp, teetering on the edge of madness. "You left me for her. After everything we did. Everything you taught me."

The words hit Layla like a physical blow, understanding crashing over her.

"You're becoming sloppy, Beatrice," Langston said, shifting his stance to position himself between the two women. "Emotional."

"Emotional?" Beatrice lunged, the scalpel flashing in the fluorescent light. "I'll show you emotional."

Langston dodged, but not fast enough. Blood bloomed across his shirt as the blade sliced through fabric and skin. He grabbed for her wrist, but she was quick, slipping free. The scalpel plunged deep into his side, and he stumbled, a guttural sound escaping his throat.

Layla rolled off the bed, tubes and wires tearing free as she hit the floor. The heart monitor let out a sustained, earsplitting flatline as she crawled toward the door, her limbs weak but driven by pure survival instinct.

Behind her, chaos erupted. Beatrice screamed—a sound of rage, pain, and betrayal. There was a wet thud, followed by another slash of the scalpel. Langston's grunt of pain turned into a sickening gurgle.

"If I can't have you," Beatrice sobbed, her voice cracking, "no one will."

Footsteps thundered in the hallway. Layla reached the doorway just as the first police officer rounded the corner, weapon drawn.

"Drop it!" the officer shouted.

Beatrice stood over Langston's crumpled body, the scalpel dripping red. Her chest heaved as she turned to meet Layla's gaze. For a moment, something passed between them—an unspoken understanding, raw and jagged. Two women, both destroyed by the same monster.

"He was mine first," Beatrice whispered, her voice empty. Then, with one swift motion, she dragged the scalpel across her throat.

The sound of her body hitting the floor sent a deafening silence through the room.

Later, they would tell Layla she was lucky. Lucky the nurse had called security. Lucky the police arrived when they did. Lucky to be alive.

But as she stood frozen in the hallway, watching the paramedics zip two body bags—one holding the man she had loved, the other the woman who had killed him—Layla wasn't sure lucky was the right word.

Six Days By: Keira N. James.

Keira N. James is a thriller author hailing from Danville, GA. While the U.S. Navy once claimed her dedication, her heart has always belonged to the world of words.

As a devoted mother raising her son, she knows that the best adventure is the one called parenthood. When she's not chasing  plot twists in her novels, Keira is raising her teenager, teaching him the ropes of becoming a productive member of society.

Keira's love affair with books started long before her writing journey began. She'd lose herself in the pages of gripping tales, and now, she's the one crafting those twists, giving readers the same excitement she once enjoyed as a bookworm.

With her dedication and determination, she's set her sights on impacting readers, providing exceptional literary experiences, and the coveted NYT Bestseller's list, and it's only a matter of time before she conquers it.

So, if you're looking for heart-pounding, page-turning suspense, Keira N. James is your go-to author. Dive into her world of thrillers and get ready for a literary escape like no other.

Day 6

The phone vibrated on the kitchen counter, buzzing against the granite like a rattlesnake's warning. Layla glanced at the screen and found 'Mom' plastered on the screen. She sat the bowl aside, brushed powdered sugar from her fingers, and answered on the third ring. "Hey, Ma. What's up?"

Silence.

"Hello?" Layla said again, furrowing her brows. Static filled the line before a faint breath was heard.

"Layla..." The voice was strained, barely a whisper, and then—nothing.

The call dropped.

Layla's chest tightened. Her mind whirled in confusion. Her mother never called without reason, and she sure as hell didn't whisper her name like she was in a damn horror movie.

Hastily, she redialed her mother's number but was sent straight to voicemail.

The warmth of the funnel cake she'd been snacking on turned sour in her mouth as she snatched up her keys from the counter, feeling her heart thud in her chest.

Something wasn't right. Nothing and no one could convince her otherwise.

The drive to her parents' house felt longer than it should've. Layla's knuckles whitened around the steering wheel, after gripping it so tight; it felt like the leather might tear.

Her playlist—usually the soothing sounds of '90s R&B— suddenly felt like static in her ears. Every lyric was drowned out by the roar of her pulse, so she killed the music because silence felt more honest and appropriate.

Trees blurred as she sped down the stretch of the oak-lined road. The sight of tall, majestic trees usually comforted her with childhood memories, but today they felt... sinister. Each oddly-twisted branch looked like a claw scratching at the sky.

Her mouth was dry, and her stomach was turning in knots, and a heavy weight pressed against her chest. The unknown had her questioning if the air was always this thick, or was it her nerves choking her from the inside out?

A flicker of movement in her peripheral vision stole her attention. It was a deer darting through the trees. The small occurrence made her heart stutter, and the sudden rush of adrenaline made her dizzy. "Get it together, Lay," she muttered.

But the unease sat heavy, refusing to be reasoned with.

Finally, after what felt like forever, she reached her mother's childhood home. Cherice had mentioned long ago that this place was where she'd come to whenever she needed to be alone. She said even Tim didn't know about it.

Layla was glad she remembered, because otherwise, she'd still be as clueless as everyone else about her mother's whereabouts.

She steered into the dirt driveway and barely shifted the car into 'park' before hopping out and darting toward the front door of the cottage-style home.

Using the spare key Cherice had given her, Layla entered the old home.

It was quiet. Almost too quiet. Like the air was holding its breath.

"Ma?" Her voice echoed in the foyer.

Cautiously, Layla stepped farther inside. The unsavory scent of musk left the cottage feeling like a ghostly echo of normalcy.

Her eyes swept over the outdated furniture in the living room. The dusty green throw pillows were still perfectly arranged. The remote was balanced on the armrest of the velvet couch, and a ceramic mug sat empty and forgotten on the cherrywood coffee table.

The refrigerator groaned from the kitchen, showing the only sign of life in the unnervingly silent house.

Layla moved forward, going from room to room as the hallway shadows tugged at her nerves, and the family photos on the walls watched her with frozen eyes.

Her throat tightened as she reached the kitchen doorway, her heart pounding against her ribs like it wanted out. She ambled inside, looking for anything out of the ordinary or something that could clue her in on her mother's whereabouts.

No sooner than she scanned the countertop, she saw Cherice's phone lying face-up with a missed call from her still glowing on the screen.

Her heart dropped to the pit of her stomach. The unsettled nerves she had when she first received the strange phone call wasn't paranoia or a result of overthinking. It was because something awful had happened to her mother. She knew it because Cherice never went anywhere or did anything without her phone.

Immediately, she started praying for her mother's safety. However, her prayers were interrupted by the faint creak of a floorboard from somewhere down the hall. Layla froze with her mouth slightly agape.

"Ma?" she called out, her voice cracking.

Brittle tension filled the air as she waited for a response.

But there was no response.

A cold draft brushed her heavily melanated skin, prompting goosebumps to pimple her arm. Her eyes darted to the back door, and she found it unlocked, open just wide enough for a shadow to slip through.

Quietly, she snatched a knife from the wooden holder, just as her phone vibrated in her pocket. She snatched it out and saw 'unknown caller rolling across the screen.

Her hands trembled as she fumbled to answer. "Hello?"

"Layla…" It was a man's voice on the line. It was smooth and familiar. "You shouldn't be here. You're only gonna make things worse."

Her throat went dry. "Who is this? Where's my mom?"

A cold chuckle came through before he answered, "Don't worry. It will all be over soon."

The line went dead.

Suddenly, the kitchen felt smaller. The temperature seemingly dropped by at least ten degrees.

The air was thick and suffocating as Layla's heart pounded in her chest. Her hand tightened around the phone as she rushed to share her location and send a '911' text to her father, Tim, who just so happened to be nearby.

Just as she pocketed her phone, a shift in the air told Layla she wasn't alone.

A sound echoed from downstairs. Her pulse quickened. She pocketed her phone and rushed toward the door leading to the basement.

She eased the door open, careful not to make too much noise, just in case she needed the element of surprise on her side. As she descended the stairs, the stale scent of mildew attacked her nostrils. A single flickering bulb overhead cast long, jagged shadows across the concrete floor, highlighting items that turned Layla's mind into a ball of confusion.

There were half-packed suitcases and scattered clothes all about the floor.

At the bottom of the stairs, she stumbled upon the last thing she ever expected to see.

Her mother. Able-bodied and well.

The world didn't make sense anymore.

"Mom? So, you were just gonna leave? You weren't really missing?" Layla's voice sliced through the tension, sharp and raw.

Cherice spun around with eyes wide with guilt. Her hand trembled on the suitcase zipper. "Layla, baby, you don't understand. I'm sorry, but this was the only way. I'm sorry you had to find out like this." Her voice, usually warm and motherly, cracked beneath the weight of her lie.

Layla stepped forward, her sneakers scuffing against the gritty floor. "No, you don't understand. How could you do this? To us? To Dad?" Her voice quivered, but her glare was steady, burning with betrayal. "We've been looking for you for days! And you've been planning to run away with this man the whole time? What kind of woman are you? What kind of mother are you?"

Bruce shifted beside Cherice, his presence towering and cold. "This ain't your business, lil' girl," he muttered, his voice deep and coated with impatience. "Your mama's made up her mind. She's leaving with me."

"It is my business," she shot back, her voice hard, slicing through the basement's chill. "You think you can just take my mom and disappear? You don't get to decide that. She has a family!"

The basement door thudded above them.

"Cherice!" Tim's voice bellowed from the stairs.

Before anyone could move, Tim burst into the room, his eyes blazing. His fists clenched at his sides, and his gaze locked on Bruce.

"You lying piece of—" he growled, and without warning, he rushed and swung at Bruce.

The crack of knuckles against flesh echoed through the small basement. Bruce staggered back into a stack of dusty boxes, sending them crashing to the floor.

"Stop it!" Cherice screamed, her voice high and broken, but the men were deaf to her pleas.

Bruce recovered fast, wiping blood from his mouth with the back of his hand. "Oh, you don' fucked up now," he snarled, his eyes flashing with something dark and dangerous. He lunged at Tim, and they collided, fists flying, grunts filling the air. They crashed into the old workbench, splintering wood and sending tools clattering about.

Layla's heart pounded so hard it hurt when she saw Bruce brandish a gun from an ankle holster.

"Stop! Please!" Her voice cracked, but her legs felt frozen.

Tim's eyes locked onto Bruce's hand. "You don't wanna do this, man," he warned, voice low and steady.

Bruce's lip curled into a snarl. "I should've killed you a long time ago," he seethed, raising the gun.

The cold weight of the moment settled into Layla's chest, pressing against her ribs.

"Bruce, wait. I'm leaving with you, baby. So, you don't have to do this," Cherice said.

True enough, she didn't love her husband anymore and had planned to run away with Bruce, but that didn't mean she wanted Timothy dead. But that didn't matter to her lover. To him, Tim was the only thing standing between them.

A gunshot cracked through the air, cutting through the thick tension like a blade.

But it wasn't Tim who fell.

Cherice gasped, her body jerking violently as the bullet tore into her.

The world seemed to move in slow motion. Layla watched in horror as her mother stumbled, her hand clutching at her stomach, crimson blooming across her pale blouse.

"Ma!" Layla's scream was raw, ripped from her throat.

Bruce's face flickered with something—shock, regret, maybe—but it vanished as quickly as it appeared. He still gripped the gun, but for the first time, his hand trembled.

Tim lunged. The two men crashed against the wall, the gun skidding across the floor.

Layla fell to her knees beside Cherice, pressing her hands over the wound, but blood seeped through her fingers.

"You're gonna be okay, Ma," Layla choked out, blinking back tears. "Just stay with me."

Cherice's lips parted— her breath shaky. "I... I just wanted to be happy," she whispered, pain lacing every word. Her fingers weakly curled around Layla's wrist, as if trying to hold on.

The sounds of the struggle barely registered in Layla's ears. All she could hear was the ragged, uneven breathing of the woman who had just thrown herself in the line of fire.

The woman who had just saved her father's life, though she had planned to leave him.

The woman who might not make it.

Tears blurred her vision as she pressed harder, desperation sinking in.

"Hold on, Ma. Please. Just hold on."

The light slowly drained from Cherice's eyes as she took her last breath.

Closer Than You Think – By: Tanisha Stewart

Award winning and bestselling author Tanisha Stewart was born and raised in Springfield, Massachusetts. She graduated with a Bachelor of Science in Psychology and Sociology in 2009, as well  as a Master of Psychology in 2011. She is a college professor, teaching psychology (which she loves). In addition to her career as a lecturer, Tanisha has been writing for as long as she can remember, creating realistic story lines, relatable characters, and multi-layered plots that almost everyone can enjoy. She also takes part in hobbies such as performing rap and spoken word for various audiences.

Tanisha not only demonstrates a passion for writing through her vivid story lines; she is also committed to helping other writers succeed. She offers author coaching, editing, formatting, and ghostwriting services to help aspiring authors get their work off the ground, and to see it through to completion. In additional to this, she hosts Book Optimization and Amazon Ads courses. You can find out more about Tanisha and these services at www.tanishastewartauthor.com.

Day 6

Layla came to, and at first everything was blurry until she slowly began to gather her bearings. A male voice echoed somewhere in the near distance, but her mind was so consumed by taking in the bright lights above her that she barely registered the words he was saying.

"Layla?"

She snapped out of it, blinking rapidly and staring in the direction of the voice until her vision and hearing became sharp and clear.

It was Langston standing by her side. Another man was standing with him, and it took a second to recognize him, but when she did, her heart faltered.

It was the attendant from the morgue.

The memories rushed back to the surface. She had come to the morgue to possibly identify her mother. When the sheet was pulled back, a woman was revealed, then everything went black.

"Layla?" Langston repeated, his forehead etched in concern. She studied him for a few moments, emotions welling within her. Tears swam to the corners of her eyes, but she refused to let them fall. Instead, she stared at him with disgust curling in her throat.

"Get the hell away from me!" she exclaimed, causing him to jump back in shock.

The attendant also looked nervous. "Ma'am?" he said. "Are you okay?"

"No, I'm not okay." Layla snarled, but she tried to keep her emotions at bay.

Langston looked confused, but Layla didn't give a damn about his feelings.

"Baby?" he said, as if unsure how to proceed.

Layla ignored him, slowly inching to a seated position. It was then that she realized she was laying on a slab like the woman she had seen earlier.

The woman who wasn't her mother.

Hot and cold prickles traveled up and down her spine as she practically leapt from the slab. "What the fuck? Why would you lay me on one of those... things?"

The attendant looked at her in puzzlement. "Ma'am, you fainted..."

"I don't give a damn what I did. You don't go laying me on a slab like I'm... Like her..." Layla said, gesturing out of the room and toward the hallway in the direction where she thought the woman might have been laying.

The attendant's lips curled into a hint of a bemused smirk, but before she could question it, his face returned to neutral.

"Take me home," she ordered Langston in a cold tone.

He stared at her. "But Layla, we haven't..."

"That woman is not my mother," she proclaimed, and both men fell into silence before they went through the motions of letting her leave.

Layla felt like she couldn't breathe until she was out of that building and into the fresh air.

At the same time, she couldn't deny the sinking feeling in her gut...

***

Back at the house, Tim awoke from his own fainting spell to the sight of Detective Vernon standing over him, a dark expression coloring his features.

Tim jerked into consciousness. "Wha... What's going on?" he stammered. "What was in that box?"

The detective's features softened slightly. "Sir, "I have something to tell you, but you need to remain calm."

"Remain calm!" Fear coursed Tim's veins. What did he mean, remain calm?

Detective Vernon spoke in an even tone, his facial expression bearing no clues of his feelings. "I have reason to believe that we may have found your wife."

Tim's fear quickly switched to elation. Giddiness escaped his throat. "What? Where is she? Where's Cherice?"

"Mr. Merriweather..." Detective Vernon started but stopped.

Tim couldn't take the suspense. "Where is my wife?" He said, quickly rising to his feet as a sense of unease settled somewhere deep within him. A small voice in the back of his head told him what he was about to hear wasn't good news, but he wasn't ready to hear it.

He preferred to see Cherice. To hold her. To kiss her. To touch her like he'd always done.

Detective Vernon didn't have to say another word. The look in his eyes destroyed any semblance of hope Tim could have mustered.

Still, he confirmed Tim's darkest fears. "I have reason to believe some of her remains were delivered in that box."

"Some of her remains!" Tim screeched his voice at a wildly unnatural octave. "What do you mean, some of her remains?"

"Mr. Merri..."

"There's no way to know it's her," Tim assured himself. "You can't know just from whatever's in that box."

Detective Vernon's next words were slow and careful. "Mr. Merriweather... From the photos you showed me the day your wife was missing... and the... particular body part that was delivered in the box... I... It's her."

"What body part?" Tim was going madder by the second. "What body part?" he repeated. "You're telling me someone... hurt her? Cut her?"

Detective Vernon didn't respond, and Tim heard footsteps walking up to his front door. Before he could ask another question, men swarmed his apartment. Men dressed in professional gear.

It was like something out of a movie.

Like a crime scene.

Before anyone could stop him, Tim raced toward the box and ripped the top open, staring at the contents before he faded to black again.

***

Layla was halfway home before she received a phone call from Detective Vernon that she almost didn't answer.

But something told her she should.

"Hello?" she said in a trembling tone, her body tense as she awaited whatever he had to say.

Langston glanced over at her from the driver's seat, still half-confused and half-pissed about how she allowed him to bring her to the morgue just to treat him in such a cold manner after she fainted.

Layla ignored his feelings and steadied her breathing as Detective Vernon confirmed her darkest suspicions, then he told her something that almost caused her world to completely crumble.

Hanging up, she turned to Langston, adrenaline coursing through her. "Turn around," she said.

"What? We just…"

"Turn around!" she said. "Get to the hospital. My dad just had a heart attack."

***

It was a grievous day for everyone involved.

Since the only part of Cherice's body that was found was the head that was delivered to Tim's home, they opted for cremation and memorial service.

Tim stared at his wife's beautiful features in the huge photo that was situated to the side of the closed and empty casket that he had rented for the day.

His eyes were on his wife, but his mind was on his daughter.

Layla refused to believe the news about her mother's passing. Her behavior had grown increasingly erratic since the story broke and there was nothing Tim could do to help her. He was overcome by his own grief.

He prayed for his daughter every day, but at night, his pillows were soaked with the tears of his own anguish.

He scanned the semi-packed sanctuary, but there was still no sign of Layla. She wasn't coming. That news struck Tim like a punch to the gut – what daughter wouldn't attend her own mother's funeral?

A sinking suspicion bubbled in the pit of his belly, but Tim squelched it. It wasn't time to start lashing out like many families did during their time of bereavement. It was time to stick together, not tear one another apart.

If Tim thought today was difficult, however, it would be nothing compared to what was in store for him. Since Cherice's death was officially ruled a homicide, the potential missing person or kidnapping case had turned into a murder case.

The only problem was, there were no leads.

Tim had been questioned until he was black and blue, as did Layla, as did Bruce, Cherice's so-called friend.

But one by one, they all were cleared. At least for now.

"Maybe that was why she didn't come," Tim muttered under his breath, then scanned the sea of faces once more for his daughter.

He didn't see her.

Six months later…

Layla was just settling back into her life.

Her mother's tragic murder would forever linger in her mind, but she had to find a way to press past her grief. Part of that process involved doing things that others might see as unnatural or unacceptable.

Layla hired a nurse to take care of her father whose health seemed to be rapidly declining since his wife's death.

She had enough to unpack with her own trauma – she didn't need to deal with his too.

Some might call her harsh for that decision, but she had to find a way to survive.

She continued with her studies and excelled in school despite the fact that she was strongly encouraged by her advisor to take a leave of absence. She refused, reasoning that diving headfirst into her future was the best way to go.

Her father wasn't the only person Layla left behind – Langston was also a thing of the past as well. Not that he had a fighting chance to get back with her anyway.

Once a cheater, always a cheater.

Layla had learned that from her mother.

There was no way she could trust Langston after what she had caught him doing with her own eyes. No excuse was good enough.

Before the anger could rise too far, Layla squelched all thoughts of depressing times, focusing on applying her makeup in the mirror.

She had a date tonight – yet another change in her life that others probably wouldn't accept, but to hell with them. They had no idea what she had been through. She deserved a shred of happiness after all the pain she suffered.

As Layla examined herself from the left side, then the right, an involuntary smile crossed her lips. She could see the light at the end of the tunnel.

Things were finally turning around for her, and she would be damned if she allowed anyone to step in her way.

A flash of a painful memory fought toward the surface of her mind, but she pushed it back and hurried down the stairs. Her heels were at the bottom of the staircase – perfect for the occasion of dinner and dancing.

Her doorbell rang as she was slipping them on.

Another smile crossed her face.

"Showtime," she said, shimmying her shoulders before a pang of guilt flashed through her. "It's not your fault," she told herself, then whipped open the door.

Detective Vernon stood on the other side, a bouquet of flowers in his hands as he greeted her with a smile.

"Shall we?" he asked, extending his arm for her to step into it.

"We shall," Layla said with a smirk, and they were on their way.

***

Tim woke up in a cold sweat, another vivid dream turned nightmare arousing him from his sleep.

He needed to talk to someone, anyone, but the good-for-nothing therapist he spoke to told him it was all in his head.

Bullshit.

Cherice was visiting him in his dreams. She had a message for him, one he needed to spread before too much time passed.

The dreams always started off good, until they took a deadly turn, and they all ended the same way. With a deadly interaction between Cherice and another person.

The problem was, Tim could never place who the person was.

They always looked and sounded familiar, but for the life of him, he couldn't break through to the truth.

If he went to the police about these dreams, they would call him crazy like his therapist did. But Tim wasn't crazy.

He knew what he'd seen. There were secrets floating around him, but if he shared them, they may do a world of harm rather than good.

***

Layla returned home exhausted after her night with Vernon. His first name was Larry, but she preferred to call him by his last name. He didn't mind it.

Vernon kissed her goodnight, then waited til she was safely inside before he walked away.

She peeked through her blinds as she watched him drive away, then smiled and turned around, only to be startled by a moving shadow that almost caused her to piss herself.

"Who's there?" she called out, her tone breathless and heart racing.

No one answered.

Layla swallowed and forced a deep breath, then inched forward, straining her ears for any hint of a sound where the shadows had come from in the kitchen.

She heard nothing.

"Hello?" she called out, but of course, there was no answer.

She kept inching closer and closer, talking to herself to keep calm with each step.

When she finally reached the throughway to the kitchen, she drew a deep breath then quickly flipped on the lights before screaming and bounding into the room, trying to catch the assailant off guard if there was one.

But there wasn't.

Just like there wasn't last time, or the time before that.

After the adrenaline died down, Layla burst into tears. "It's not my fault..." she croaked, but the more she said it, the less she believed it.

Six months ago...

The phone felt heavy in her hand as she stared at the text she'd just sent. Her mother would receive it any minute now - proof of her infidelity captured in grainy photos through a car window. Layla's hands trembled as she waited in the shadows of the empty park, fallen leaves crunching beneath her feet as she shifted her weight.

When headlights swept across the entrance, her heart lurched. Her mother's silver sedan pulled in slowly, hesitantly, like a wounded animal sensing a trap. Layla watched from behind a thick oak tree as her mother emerged, wrapped in that cream cashmere sweater she always wore when she was nervous.

"I'm here," her mother called out, voice sharp with false bravado. "Show yourself."

Layla stepped out, and the look of shock that crossed her mother's face would haunt her forever.

"Layla? What is this?" Her mother's expression morphed from surprise to anger. "You're blackmailing me now?"

"I saw you, Mom. With Bruce." The words tasted bitter. "How could you do this to Dad?"

"You followed me?" Her mother's laugh was harsh, unfamiliar. "You little spy. This is none of your business."

"None of my business? You're destroying our family!"

"Oh, grow up, Layla. The world isn't black and white. You have no idea what goes on in a marriage."

"I know right from wrong," Layla spat, stepping closer. "And what you're doing is wrong."

Her mother turned away with a dismissive wave. "I'm not having this conversation with my child. Stay out of grown folks' business."

The dismissive gesture ignited something in Layla. She lunged forward, grabbing her mother's arm. "Don't you walk away from me!"

Her mother spun around, eyes flashing with a fury Layla had never seen before. "Take your hands off me!" She shoved Layla hard enough to make her stumble backward.

The rage that had been simmering beneath the surface exploded. Layla recovered her balance and charged forward, shoving back with all her might. "How dare you-"

The words died in her throat as her mother's heel caught on an exposed tree root. Time seemed to slow as she watched her mother's arms windmill, trying to catch her balance. But there was nothing to grab onto. Her head struck the rock with a sound Layla would never forget - a dull crack that seemed to echo through the empty park.

"Mom?" Her voice came out small, like a child's. "Mom, get up."

But her mother didn't move.

Layla dropped to her knees beside her, hands hovering uncertainly over her mother's still form. "Mom, please. I'm sorry. Please get up." When she finally worked up the courage to touch her mother's neck, searching for a pulse, the skin was already growing cool.

"No, no, no..." The word became a mantra as she paced in circles, pulling at her hair. This couldn't be happening. This wasn't real. But every time she looked back, her mother was still there, sprawled unnaturally on the ground, eyes staring sightlessly at the night sky.

Her phone felt like it weighed a thousand pounds as she pulled it out with trembling hands. She scrolled through her contacts until she found the one person she knew who could handle something like this.

"Vernon? I need help. Please... I've done something terrible."

Vernon's silence on the other end of the line felt eternal. Finally, his gravelly voice came through. "Where are you?"

Layla gave him the location, her voice barely a whisper. "Please hurry."

When he arrived, his eyes scanned the area, ensuring no one else was in sight. Then he immediately launched into action. "Listen carefully," he said. "Take her car to Sawyer's Ridge. The steep part, where there's no guardrail. Put it in neutral and let it go over. Then get yourself to the gas station on Route 16 and call a ride service. Go home and stay there. Don't call anyone else. Don't come back here. I'll handle the rest."

"Wait," Layla grabbed his arm, her voice cracking. "My dad... he needs to know what happened to her. Not this, but something. He can't spend the rest of his life wondering."

Vernon was quiet for a moment. "I'll handle that too. But it'll cost you."

"Anything," she whispered. "I'll pay anything."

She forced herself to walk to her mother's car, parked just beyond the trees. Her mother's keys were still in her pocket, where she'd snatched them after... after. Her hands trembled as she unlocked the door. The familiar scent of her mother's perfume hit her as she slid behind the wheel, and she had to fight back a wave of nausea.

The drive to Sawyer's Ridge felt endless. Every passing car made her heart stop, certain it was someone who would see her, would know what she'd done. When she finally reached the spot Vernon had mentioned, she sat there for a long moment, car idling, staring into the darkness beyond the ridge.

"I'm sorry," she whispered, though she wasn't sure who she was apologizing to anymore. Then she put the car in neutral, stepped out, and watched as it rolled forward, picking up speed until it disappeared over the edge. The crash, when it came, seemed too distant to be real...

Still trembling from her encounter with the shadows, Layla sank onto her couch, remembering the night six months ago when Vernon had called her, asking to meet for dinner. She'd been terrified, certain he was going to demand an exorbitant amount of money. Instead, he'd taken her to an intimate restaurant two towns over, where no one would recognize them.

"I've always found you intriguing," he'd said, his dark eyes studying her over the rim of his wine glass. "But you never gave me the time of day before."

She nearly choked on her water. "What?"

"Now we share something special," he continued, reaching across the table to touch her hand. "A bond that no one else could understand. Why not see where it leads?"

The irony wasn't lost on her - falling for the very detective assigned to solve her mother's murder. Every time she saw him, at first, her stomach would twist into knots. But he always steered the investigation away from her, subtle enough that no one would notice.

Six months of secret meetings, stolen kisses in darkened parking lots, and whispered conversations. Now that the case had gone cold, they could finally be seen together in public. She and Vernon had even shared the news with her father last week, and Tim reacted surprisingly well, shaking Vernon's hand and thanking him for all his hard work trying to find out what happened to his wife.

Layla pulled her knees to her chest, trying to stop shaking. The shadows in her house seemed to grow longer, darker. Sometimes she wondered if this was Vernon's plan all along - to have something to hold over her head forever. Other times, when he held her close and whispered how much he loved her, she almost believed they could have a real future together.

But nights like tonight, when the shadows moved and guilt clawed at her throat, she knew better. She was living on borrowed time, dancing on the edge of a cliff. One day, someone would find out. One wrong word, one slip-up, and everything would come crashing down.

***

Tim rocked slowly in his chair, the worn wood creaking beneath him like old bones. The porch light attracted moths that danced in endless circles, reminding him of how his thoughts kept spinning around the same dark center.

Cherice's face haunted his dreams again last night. "You know what you saw, Timothy," she'd whispered, her features sharp with urgency. "Stop pretending you don't."

He closed his eyes, feeling the weight of the yearbook in his lap. He'd brought it down from the attic weeks ago, and now he couldn't stop looking at it. There they were - Layla Merriweather and Larry Vernon, just a few rows apart in their graduating class. Vernon's face was younger, but that same calculated look was there in his eyes, even then.

The memory of Mother Davidson's phone call made his hands shake as they gripped the armrests. "I wasn't sure if I should say anything, Tim, but I saw them at that new Italian place in Riverdale. They looked... intimate."

His daughter and the detective investigating his wife's murder. His daughter and her old classmate. The pieces were there, like a jigsaw puzzle he was too afraid to complete.

Layla hadn't hugged him since Cherice died. She used to throw her arms around him every time she visited, but now she kept her distance, as if afraid he might feel her guilt through her skin. And the way she looked at him sometimes, when she thought he wasn't watching - like she was searching for something in his face, measuring how much he knew.

The rocking chair creaked louder as Tim leaned forward, staring into the darkness beyond his porch. He remembered how

Layla had been tight with concern because her mother hadn't come home. He'd thought nothing of it then. But now...

"I know you're trying to tell me something, Cherice," he whispered to the night air. "But what am I supposed to do with it?"

The truth was, he was afraid of the answer. Afraid that if he pulled this thread, his whole world would unravel. His was gone, and now he might lose Layla too. But the weight of not knowing, of pretending not to see what was right in front of him, was slowly killing him.

Tim reached into his pocket and pulled out the business card he'd been carrying for days. Robert Chen, Private Investigator. He'd found him online, someone from two counties over who wouldn't know anyone involved.

"Give me a sign, Cherice," he whispered, turning the card over in his trembling hands. "Tell me what to do."

A sudden gust of wind swept across the porch, scattering the moths and sending the yearbook sliding from his lap. It fell open on the wooden boards, pages ruffling until they settled. Tim leaned down slowly, his joints protesting, and picked it up.

It had fallen open to the senior quotes page. Right there, under Vernon's picture, were the words that made Tim's blood run cold: The perfect crime isn't the one that goes unsolved - it's the one where everyone thinks they know what happened.

Tim reached for his phone.

With Friends Like These – By: Kenya Moss-Dyme

Kenya has been crafting stories since elementary school when her first book - the story of a cricket longing to be an astronaut - was  placed in the school library for others to check out. It wasn't until many years later, however, that she wrote her first full length horror story, Patchwork, detailing a scorned wife taking revenge on her ex-husband. Fast forward to 2013 when she took the opportunity to publish Prey for Me, the tale of a monstrous child-abusing preacher; followed by the twisted romance series, A Good Wife. As a multi-genre writer whose work most often leans into horror, Kenya recognizes that the real monsters are inside of us all and you will find a bit of darkness in everything she writes.

Day 6

Standing at the kitchen counter, Tim stared blankly through the window into the backyard. He looked unkempt, dirty and exhausted, and felt even worse. Bloodshot eyes peered out of an unshaven face that showed wrinkles he had never noticed before...before Cherice *left*. In the background, the television played the local news, softly narrating his current nightmare.

"Police continue to search for forty-three-year-old Cherice Merriweather, reported missing this past Tuesday morning. Merriweather was last seen by her husband at their Oakwood residence the previous evening. Authorities and the Merriweather family are asking anyone with information to please come forward."

Tim sighed and grabbed the remote from the counter to mute the television. He couldn't bear to hear it again and again, and again. That clinical description of his wife reduced to an age, a name, and a last known location, as if 25 years of marriage could be easily squished into a thirty-second sound bite.

"Pops?"

Tim turned to face Layla standing in the doorway. Her face was gaunt, her hair pulled up to the top of her head into a messy knot. She still wore the same hoodie she'd been wearing when they discovered Cherice had disappeared, as if changing clothes would somehow be admitting that life was continuing in her mother's absence.

"Any news since I went to the store and came back?" Layla asked, her voice soft, full of pain but also edged with her customary sarcasm. She'd decided not to mention her earlier visit to the morgue, especially since it didn't provide any answers.

Tim shook his head. "Nothing new. Detective Vernon said he'd stop by this afternoon with an update."

Layla nodded, moving to the refrigerator and opening it, only to close it again without taking anything out. She'd been doing that repeatedly over the past three days—going through the motions of normalcy without actually following through.

"I made some flyers," she said, waving her hand toward a stack of papers on the dining table. "I thought I could put them up around downtown."

The flyers featured a smiling Cherice, her eyes crinkled at the corners, showing no signs of any turmoil that might have been brewing deep in her mind. Below the image, in bold letters: MISSING. The sight of his wife's face made Tim's chest tighten.

Layla kept opening and closing her mouth, seemingly gathering herself to say something more.

"Do you think... do you think she's okay?" Her voice cracked on the final word.

Tim set his mug down with more force than intended, coffee splashing over the rim. "She has to be," he said firmly. "We're going to find her."

Detective Vernon showed up at the door again, interrupting the unspoken questions hanging in the air between them. Layla groaned, rolling her eyes as she watched him on the Ring app at their front door. This Columbo act was beginning to wear on her, but she couldn't let him see that his presence was a bother. After all, his job was to find her mother, and they all had the same goal, right?

"Mr. Vernon." She opened the door, and he looked surprised.

Behind her, Tim entered the living room and plopped down on the sofa, hands clasped tightly in his lap, waiting for the anticipated update. Vernon took a seat in the armchair across from him and pulled out a folder.

"I just wanted to touch base with you both in person," he began. "I've been following up on several leads, but this one in particular stood out."

He flipped through the pages and stopped, pointing his finger toward a line of data.

"The phone records came in. Look here, she called someone named Regina Miller at approximately 7:30 pm Monday."

Layla's head snapped up. "Regina? Mom called Regina?"

Detective Vernon nodded, studying Layla's reaction. "You know Ms. Miller?"

"She's Mom's coworker, well, she used to be before Mom quit," Layla explained. "They've known each other for years. Did you talk to her?"

"We did," Detective Simmons confirmed. "Ms. Miller said she didn't hear from your mother on Monday. But the phone records clearly show a call was made. And when I went back to see how often they spoke -" He flipped back through the previous pages. "-It looks like they're pretty close, talking almost daily. Yet, no one ever mentioned her during all of our investigations."

Layla shook her head. "Because I never would have imagined them talking that frequently, especially since Mom no longer worked with her. They were cool but not *that* cool."

Tim frowned. "Regina wouldn't lie about something like that."

"How would you know if she would lie? We don't know her like that!" Layla insisted. Tim looked down at the carpet while Detective Vernon made a note in the margin of the paper.

"We'll follow up with Ms. Miller again. People lie, phone records don't."

He turned his attention back to Layla. "You are still the last person to see your mother. Can you tell me about your last conversation with her?

"I don't understand why that's important," Layla replied defensively.

"Layla! Anything you can recall could help find her!" Tim shot back.

Layla began to twist her hands together nervously. "We... we had an argument," she finally admitted. "I noticed money missing from my bank account—almost a thousand dollars. We linked accounts for emergencies, and I saw transfers going to her account."

"You accused your mother of taking money from you?" the detective asked, his tone neutral but his eyes sharp.

"I asked her about it," Layla corrected. "She denied it. Said she hadn't touched my account. But the evidence was right there on the app. We argued about it. I..." She hesitated, tears welling in her eyes. "I told her she needed to get checked for memory loss. That maybe she was doing things and forgetting them. She got really upset and left the house."

"What time was this?"

"Around seven," Layla said. "I was so mad, I didn't mean to say that to her, but it just slipped out..."

Tim looked at his daughter in surprise. "You never told me about the money."

"I was going to," Layla said. "But then Mom disappeared, and it seemed so trivial compared to that."

Detective Vernon continued making notes. "And what time did you return home?"

"Around nine," Layla said. "I thought Mom would be back by then, but she wasn't. I texted her too, apologizing for what I said."

"I'll be honest with you, the first forty-eight hours are crucial, and we're past that point. The fact that her car and phone are also missing tells me that she may have left voluntarily, but no activity since Monday is concerning."

"What are you saying?" Tim asked, a tremor in his voice.

"I'm saying we're expanding our search and treating this as a potential foul play situation," Detective Vernon replied gently. "Her banking records show no activity, her phone hasn't pinged any towers since Monday evening, and none of her friends have heard from her."

"Except Regina," Layla interjected. "The phone records show Mom called her."

Detective Vernon nodded. "Oh, don't worry. I'll be speaking with Ms. Miller again today."

After the detective left, Tim and Layla sat in uncomfortable silence; Tim leaned his elbows on his knees and sighed while Layla held her breath waiting for him to speak.

"Why didn't you tell me about the money?" he said finally.

Layla wiped at the tears that broke free. "I was gonna sort it out with Mom first."

"And you really think your mother took it?" Tim asked in disbelief.

"The transfers came from her account! What was I supposed to think?"

Tim shook his head. "Your mother wouldn't do that. There has to be some explanation."

"Well, she's not here to give one, is she?" Layla snapped, then immediately looked ashamed. "I'm sorry. I didn't mean that. I'm just scared. What if something happened to her because of our stupid fight?"

"Don't do that. This isn't your fault. She's probably hiding out in a hotel room trying to make you worry so you'll feel bad."

But even as he said the words, a creeping doubt gnawed at him. What if they didn't find her? What if Cherice was...

He couldn't bring himself to finish the thought.

Earlier (The Morgue)

Choking back tears, Layla pushed open the exit door, clutched the stair railing for support, and then lowered herself to sit on the front steps of the building. The wind blew against her face, and she closed her eyes, inhaling deeply. She felt the tension start to leave her neck and shoulders, and the pounding in her temples subsided.

Suddenly, Langston appeared, bending his long legs to sit on the cold concrete stair next to her. He wrapped her in his arms, pulling her into a warm and comforting hug. Feeling safe again, Layla released the tears.

"It's okay, babe," Langston whispered as he rubbed her back.

Several minutes passed before she was able to compose herself and withdraw from his arms.

"I've never done that before-" Layla said, wiping her face as she noticed another set of visitors approaching the stairs with solemn faces.

"I know. Neither have I."

"That was truly awful. That poor woman - whoever she is, someone loved her."

Langston nodded. "Well, now that we know it's not Cherice, some other family can get closure."

"But we still don't know where Mom is. A part of me was hoping that was her, you know? Then another part of me is happy it wasn't."

"That's completely understandable," Langston protectively covered her hand with his as another couple walked up the stairs into the building.

"Let's get out of here, I can't stand to sit here and see all of these people about to possibly see their loved ones...like that."

She allowed him to pull her to her feet and they walked hand in hand back to the car.

It may have been a little early for wine, but Regina Miller sat in her living room unapologetically sloshing a deep red cabernet around the bowl of a wine glass. Her face set in a hardened frown as she squinted her eyes and tilted her head trying to sort things out in her mind. Her thoughts were murky, and her mind foggy as she watched the seconds tick slowly by. The house was quiet, almost too quiet, except for the dog barking outside in her driveway.

Regina sank deeper into the cushions of her sofa, ignoring the building sense of panic that churned deep in her gut. The loud, rhythmic barking kept pulling her back out of the trance and she knew eventually it would annoy someone enough to come over to investigate. The damn thing had been at it all morning— pacing back and forth, agitated and snarling at her door.

The wine helped take the edge off. But as the hours passed, the dog was still angry and each bark felt as if it were chiseling along the edges of her brain, slowly chipping away at the facade of peace. Someone should have noticed by now and come to get it. The noise was driving her insane, but Regina knew she had to stay focused on her thoughts and not spin out of control.

It wasn't even her dog.

The unruly beast they called King had squeezed through a hole in the neighbor's fence, not quite unexpectedly, since he did that often. King would come over, sniff, and leave. But this time, King wasn't leaving until he got some answers.

They say dogs can smell the dead.

Clearly, if she wanted to get rid of King, she was going to have to do something about that body in the basement.

****

Earlier, King came sauntering over to nuzzle Cherice when she stepped out of her car. Regina hadn't expected Cherice to actually come over, but she was so distraught when she called, the invitation just spilled out of her mouth before she even thought it through.

"You don't know that dog!" Regina scoffed. "Don't touch it."

"She just wants to say hello," Cherice cooed at the German Shepherd, holding still so the dog could nuzzle against her leg.

"Yuck." Regina shook her head and turned to unlock her door. "You gonna stay out here with that animal or you coming inside so we can crack open this bottle?"

They say that dogs can sense good people, Regina chuckled softly as she watched King completely turn into a sweet natured pet as Cherice stroked its ear. Of course she could soothe it with her charm; she had that effect on people.

Another reason Regina hated her guts.

Cherice was perfect. So damn perfect Regina hated her guts from the moment they'd become coworkers at the cellphone store.

Regina was a technician, while Cherice worked sales upfront at the counter. Her smile and pleasant demeanor soothed the customers and kept them calm even when delivering the worse news about their bills and accounts.

Regina's official title was Mobile Solution Expert, but unofficially, she was the rooting expert aka jailbreak specialist. When customer support couldn't provide the solution, Regina could. Customers knew to slip a hundred-dollar bill or two into her hand and let her spend a few minutes in the back with their phones and she would fix whatever issue they were having.

That's how she was able to hack into Cherice's phone and clone it so that she could read all of Cherice's messages and emails and basically spy on her 24/7. The lovey-dovey messages between Cherice and Tim were sickening. That man loved her so much that even the smallest complaint from her about being tired or needing to sit down, lead to him pleading with her to quit her job and stay home so he could take care of her. It just wasn't fair that she had this kind of love and Regina had no one to love her, not even a cat.

She would sit at home and scroll through Cherice's life and feel the hate burning inside her belly like an inferno.

Making the secret transfers from Layla's bank account was the win she never imagined. At first, it was funny, and she cackled to herself as she withdrew a thousand here and there, depositing it into her own account and then deleting the records so Cherice would have no clue. But the morning she called in tears after a blowup with Layla over the money, Regina had to put her on mute while she howled with laughter at her friend's distress. It gave her all of the feels. Fuck that bitch. She deserved every second of sadness because who did she think she was? Why did she deserve to have such a grand life while Regina had nothing but bad luck?

Sighing loudly, Regina stood on shaky legs and walked to the television, turning the volume up just in time to hear the newscaster report on Cherice being missing. The station wasn't letting this one go; it was as if Cherice Merriweather were the only woman in the world to have ever gone missing. Regina turned the volume up louder to drown out King's barking, but the combination of the wine, the barking, and now Tim crying on television enraged her.

"Fifty-three-year-old Cherice Merriweather has not been seen or heard from for over a week. Her family insists she didn't leave willingly, but police say her car and phone are also missing. If you have any information, you are asked to contact authorities immediately."

They showed the same photo every time—Cherice smiling, radiant, her dark hair framing her face perfectly.

Regina picked up her glass and took a long final sip before stumbling into the kitchen to withdraw the sharpest knife from the butcher block. Killing Cherice didn't give her the high she wanted, she needed more. She spotted an empty box in the corner from a shipment of cellphones, it was just large enough for her plan for one last hurrah to really get her point across. She lined the inside of the box with a trash bag, then retrieved some leftover steak from the fridge to entice the beast outside.

They say German Shepherds are smart. King, not so much. He wanted to get inside, so inside he was going to get.

****

An hour later, Regina was driving drunk, pulling away from the house in Cherice's car with a body in the back seat wrapped tightly in the latest mummy fashion. She didn't plan on going too far. The lake was just over a mile away, so she drove slowly, purposefully, hoping not to attract attention. Just a few more minutes and it would all be over and she could get back home and sleep off the buzz.

A courier would be delivering the box soon to Cherice's perfect husband. Regina laughed out loud as she imagined the horror on his face when he opened it. She only wished she was there to witness it. Serves his ass right for ignoring her every time he came into the store to take Cherice out to lunch or - gag - bring her lunch. He was so in love; he didn't even notice her. She was prettier than Cherice, her body was better than Cherice's, and she was smarter than Cherice. Fuck that man. She hoped he enjoyed his present.

Regina's resentment had grown over the years like a tumor she couldn't excise. But today was the day she would finally be free!

The sun was starting to set by the time she pulled up to the lake bank, and it was thankfully empty of any other visitors. They were usually sitting around fishing or walking, or just staring into the water, but this time, she was the only person there. It was fate indeed.

****

With a backup squad car following close behind, Detective Vernon drove as fast as he could toward Regina Miller's address. He contemplated using the siren to clear the traffic, something he rarely got the chance to do, but he also didn't want to alert her to his approach. Since leaving the Merriweather home earlier, every lead pointed to Ms. Miller as not only the main person of interest in Cherice's disappearance but also hinted that she may potentially be dangerous. Her outright lie about not speaking to Cherice was the first clue that she needed to be looked at more closely, because the cell phone records showed daily conversations and text messages as if they were the closest friends. Transcripts of the text messages were on the way, but a trip to the retail store where the women worked was all he needed to confirm his suspicion.

Initially, Jeff the store manager was accommodating and answered each of Detective Vernon's questions without hesitation. The store was busy with customers, so he took the detective to the back office so they could speak discreetly. He confirmed that Cherice had worked there in the past and that Regina was a current employee at the store. According to Jeff, she was their top device technician, able to perform high level operations such as recovering lost data and - how had he put it? Cracking, that's what he called it, he said with a laugh, she could crack *any* phone. The interview took a sharp left turn however, when the detective asked about her friendship with Cherice.

"Friends?" Jeff exclaimed, his eyes wide. "They weren't friends. Regina hated her guts! I'm pretty sure they haven't crossed paths since Cherice's husband retired her."

Jotting down notes as fast as he could, the detective's stomach turned into knots as the manager continued.

"If you ask me, Regina was just a little bit jealous, that's what I think," added Jeff.

Moments later, Detective Vernon was calling for backup and speeding toward Regina's residence to question and possibly place her under arrest, and hopefully, bring Cherice home to her family.

****

Her plan was to sink the body, weight it down with rocks, and watch it sink until only the ripples remained. But in her drunken stupor, she failed to put the car into Park as she stepped out of the Driver's side door. She could do nothing but watch it roll down the embankment and submerge itself into the water. For a moment, she stood frozen on the shore, the shock of what she'd just witnessed immobilizing her. After the top of the car disappeared beneath the surface, Regina finally shrugged and accepted that maybe this change of plan was actually better. Now she didn't have to worry about hiding the car, but she did have to stumble back home in the darkness and clean up the mess she'd left.

With a deep sigh, she turned and began the trek back up the embankment, heading toward the road.

Next time, not too much on the wine, she mumbled out loud, then laughed. *Next time?*

Although her reflexes were dulled by the wine, she managed to walk a couple of miles in the dark, but when she stepped out of the tree line and into the road, the headlights of Detective Vernon's SUV barreled down upon her. There was no time to react, brake or swerve; the truck snatched her beneath the grill and the underbody tore her to shreds. The police car behind him ran off the road, coming to a halt just before crashing into the trees.

By the time Detective Vernon was able to regain control of the steering wheel and bring the truck to a stop, Regina was long gone— taking all of her secrets with her.

Dear Readers,

We want to take a moment to express our sincere gratitude for choosing to read this work. Your support means the world to us, and we truly appreciate the time you've invested in exploring these words.

If you enjoyed the book and found it valuable, we kindly ask you to leave a review. Your feedback is invaluable not only to us but also to fellow readers who are looking for their next great read. Your honest thoughts can make a significant difference and help others discover the story within these pages.

Thank you once again for your support. We are deeply grateful for every reader who joins us on this literary journey.

www.ingramcontent.com/pod-product-compliance
Lightning Source LLC
Chambersburg PA
CBHW061212170626
46809CB00003B/1332